LET SLEEPING DOGS LIE

LET SLEEPING DOGS LIE

HELAINE BECKER

ILLUSTRATED BY JENN PLAYFORD

ORCA BOOK PUBLISHERS

Library and Archives Canada Cataloguing in Publication

Becker, Helaine, 1961–, author
Let sleeping dogs lie / Helaine Becker.
(Dirk Daring, secret agent)

Issued in print and electronic formats.
ISBN 978-1-4598-1038-9 (pbk.).—ISBN 978-1-4598-1039-6 (pdf).—
ISBN 978-1-4598-1040-2 (epub)

I. Title.
PS8553.E295532L48 2015   jc813'.6   C2015-904478-2
C2015-904479-0

First published in the United States, 2016
Library of Congress Control Number: 2015944490

Summary: In this middle-grade novel and sequel to *Dirk Daring, Secret Agent*, Darren Dirkowitz and his associates must embark on a daring mission to outsmart a gang of teen thugs known as the Wolf Lords.

MIX
Paper from
responsible sources
FSC® C016245
www.fsc.org

Orca Book Publishers is dedicated to preserving the environment and has printed this book on Forest Stewardship Council® certified paper.

Orca Book Publishers gratefully acknowledges the support for its publishing programs provided by the following agencies: the Government of Canada through the Canada Book Fund and the Canada Council for the Arts, and the Province of British Columbia through the BC Arts Council and the Book Publishing Tax Credit.

Design and illustrations by Jenn Playford
Author photo by Karl Szasz

www.orcabook.com
Printed and bound in Canada.

19 18 17 16 • 4 3 2 1

DON'T TELL ANYONE, BUT THIS CLASSIFIED DOCUMENT IS DEDICATED TO AGENT AMY, WHO UNCOVERED ITS SECRETS.

Preparatory Training Mission 12
Case Report 71 De-encrypted. Cell Block. 1/9.

Down. Stay.

The cell was bright, hot and bright. It stank of stale sweat and graphite—the potent pong of panic and capitulation.

Blazing lights blinded me. The hard slat of the chairback wracked my spine. It mattered not. Mere discomfort could not distract me. I had just one task now—to conceal all. To wall all.

I could just make out my interrogator. A she-wolf straight from the Russian steppe. "Mrs. Gudonov."

No, she was *not* good enough. Not to get the better of me—Dirk Daring, Secret Agent.

She shifted her wolfish eyes. Left, right, left, right. Twitched her wolfish nose, left, right, left, right. I'd give her nothing to sink her fangs into. *Nyet*—not yet.

Slap! A blank sheet of paper hit the desk in front of me.

Slap! A blue ballpoint pen materialized beside it.

The tools to write out my "confession."

"You know the drill," Gudonov barked. "Put your deets on the top line. Now."

I wrote.

Name.

Rank.

Serial number.

Then I put down my pen.

She of the lupine eye and canine tooth wouldn't get her paws on a single kibble-bit of info more. Not from this puppy.

There was too much at stake.

The hot light scorched my face, my eyes. Beads of sweat balled up like little BBs on the back of my neck. The fabric of my standard-issue trousers stuck to my thighs.

I was thirsty too—doggone thirsty! And light-headed from lack of food, sunlight, sleep...

Even so, my thoughts were not for myself. Never just for myself. I thought instead of my *compadres*, who, like me, were confined in this stinking prison. Each in their own private hell, facing the same torture.

Would *they* break?

No! I assured myself. They would not. Hadn't I trained them personally?

My interlocutor rapped a yardstick against the flaking cinderblock.

She snarled, "Question 1: Identify this land formation."

The inside of my eyelids felt like garnet sandpaper. My eyeballs, like eggs on the boil. Despite my agony, I could just make out a photographic image flickering on the wall.

It depicted a distinctive land mass. Very distinctive.

I suppressed a tremor of disquiet. *Did she already know something?*

"Answer 1: Florida. A peninsula," I wrote. "Bounded on three sides by water."

She barked again. "Question 2: Identify *this* land formation."

A second image flashed on the cinderblock. In my brain, a corresponding image flared.

Another tremor roiled in my gut.

Mere coincidence? Or—

Did she know…?

I wrote, "Answer 2: Panama. An isthmus. A land bridge joining two larger land masses."

I did *not* write that I had received a message from our agent there (code name Orlando). Just two weeks earlier. Confirming my upcoming mission…

A third image flashed. Then a fourth and a fifth. A pattern emerged.

It was unmistakable.

A seismic collage of truth.

Not coincidence, then.

I answered the rest of Gudonov's questions with cool, calm calculation. But truth be told, fear—that emotion heretofore unknown to me—had begun to germinate in the disturbed turf of my gut. A dark watermelon seed of uh-oh…

A final image flashed before my eyes.

This one, a set of longitudinal and latitudinal coordinates.

43.72765° N, 79.402721° W.

Yes, I knew them. Like the back of my hand.

I put down my pen.

I could not deflect or deceive. Not any longer.

Yet Dirk Daring, Secret Agent, would never confirm what was located at those very coordinates.

"You do not know the answer?" Gudonov *grrrred*. Undeterred. Undefeated.

"I do not," I purred. Unbowed. Unbroken.

Gudonov stared at the pen, lying flat on the desk. At my hands, lying clasped in my lap. At my eyes, lying straight to her face.

She whisked the paper from my desk. Gave me a thin-lipped, lupine smile.

"You may go. But remember—I have my eye on you, young man."

I thanked her, oh so politely. Tipped an imaginary hat at her. Even tossed her an insouciant wink as I slipped from the cell.

In the shadowy corridors, though, I fell back against the wall. Pressed my hand to my chest. Felt my heart galumphing like a mad burro.

The door opened again. Another agent emerged. One of mine.

She was pale, drawn.

"Was it very bad for you?" Her voice, a papery whisper.

I nodded. "You?"

She gave a false laugh. "Let's just say geography isn't my best subject. If I passed, it will only be by a whisker."

A wolf's whisker, I thought.

We emerged together into the deceptive, bright clarity of afternoon. We held her lie—*a geography test!*—between us like a lifeline.

A life *lie.*

If only it were true! I would have capered with delight at the sweet simplicity of it all!

But I, Dirk Daring, knew better.

We had not taken a simple school examination.

We had been given a message.

They knew who we were.

They knew where to find us.

And *they* were on their way.

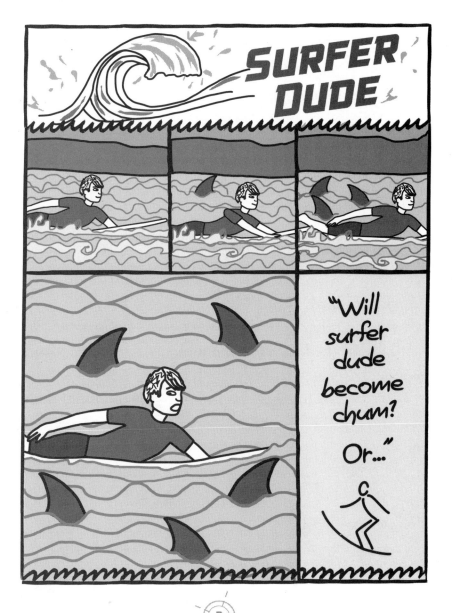

Opal grumbled, "I don't know why you keep calling it a *Kitchen Cabinet* meeting. When we're not, you know, actually in the kitchen." She looked around the room pointedly, letting her eye rest on Jason's rumpled sheets.

Jason shook his head mournfully. "You are, sadly, such a literal creature. So young. So painfully unschooled in history."

JASON ARSENICO
AKA AGENT WALDO
AKA THE STEP-BROTHER

Identifying Physical Features

Five o'clock shadow

Zit constellation
(Ursa Major) on chin

Evil glint in eye

Assets: High government position. Access to authority, budgets. Smarm and charm. Low cunning. Not afraid to use physical power to reach desired outcome.

Liabilities: Big head/ego. Minimal intelligence. Offensive personal habits. Prone to gas.

Previous Missions:

☆ Two Bird One Stone

☆ Re-Treat

☆ Go Fish

Status:

On assignment

"Uh-oh, he's going into lecture mode! Dive for cover! Dive for cover!" I shouted. I threw myself toward the bed but thought better of it. Knowing Jason's personal habits and all.

I did a seriously awkward midair jackknife, came down like a twisted pretzel on the carpet and clonked my head on the corner of the desk.

Jason hooted. "Serves you right. For being such a toolbag." He turned to Opal. "And for your information, Miss La-di-da, a Kitchen Cabinet is the nickname for a president's group of informal advisors. As opposed to, you know, the official cabinet. And since I am Student Council president, and you dweebles are apparently my informal advisors, that makes you my Kitchen Cab—"

Lucinda patted me on the back. "You were right. We all should have dove for cover. *Dove*—that's 8 points."

LUCINDA LEE
AKA AGENT FURY
AKA THE UNICORN

Identifying Physical Features

• Calculating glint in eye

• Flowy black "unicorn mane"

• Hello Kitty barrette

Assets: Math skills. Code-writing/breaking skills. Surveillance skill. Blackmail ability

Liabilities: Some serious insecurity issues. Prone to fantasy, giggling, doodling hearts, flowers. Obsession with Sudoku, Scrabble, Crosswords, Battleship

Previous Missions: **Status:** Active

✿ Independent Black ops – Waldo Blackmail

✿ Cat Flap-Up

✿ Go Fish

"Or *dived*. Ten points. Or simply *plugged our ears*," Opal said.

Assets: Extreme intelligence. Admirable cunning. Access to enemy agents (Double Trouble). Superior strategic-planning skills. Superior ability to camouflage herself and sneak into enemy territory unseen. Awesome creative-writing skills. Pretty and incredibly charming.

Liabilities: None.   **Status:** Active

Previous Missions:

☆ T-Bone Stake

☆ Cat Flap-Up

☆ Go Fish

"Hey, you are all free to leave." Jason indicated the door with a sweep of his hand. "But then you won't have the unique access to the inner secrets of Student Council, will you?"

"And you won't have our help. Which you need. Desperately." I jerked my finger toward the newsprint dodecahedron on Jason's desk. It was a badly crumpled copy of the *Preston Prestige*. This week's cover story was about Jason's popularity falling—*diving*—in the school polls.

SPY CELL STRUCTURE

Case Officer/ Cell Spymaster
AGENT 001: Dirk Daring

Reports to...?

COVER STORY

Unofficial advisory group (AKA Kitchen Cabinet) to Preston School President Jason Arsenico

Deputy Case Officer
AGENT 002: Jewel
Areas of expertise:
A3: Strategy
A4: Logistics
A2: Covert Surveillance

AGENT 003: Waldo
Areas of expertise:
A6: Intelligence gathering
A12: Public relations

AGENT 004: Fury
Areas of expertise:
A2: Covert surveillance
A7: Codes

AGENT 005: T-Bone
DEACTIVATED
Areas of expertise:
ALL

We stared at each other. Hard eye to hard eye.

Jason broke first. Naturally.

"So shall we continue?" he said.

"Yeah. I have to practice for the district Scrabble tournament," Lucinda said.

"We know. Just around the corner. You've told us," Opal said. "Like, a bil times."

"Uh-huh. So let's get C-R-A-C-K-I-N-G. Which is... hmmm...16 points, plus 50 for using seven letters... that's...66 reasons to hurry!"

"You are so weird," Opal said with a laugh. "Which is why we love you. I think."

Lucinda's own grin bared her new pink-and-purple braces. "D-I-T-T-O. Six points."

Jason waved a sheet of paper in our faces. "People? Agenda?"

"Go for it," I said.

"Bonaparte is apoplectic."

"Ooh! Apoplectic! Good word!" Lucinda started counting out its Scrabble value on her fingers. "One, four..."

"He got some cataclysmic news."

"...five, eight..."

"Which means, for you young, woefully limited grade fives, that it's really, really bad." Jason brought his forehead to the heel of his hand. "It will change our lives forever."

"Cut the drama and get to the point already," Opal said.

Jason tipped his head toward the door. "Feel free."

"Eighteen!" Lucinda shouted.

Jason shot her a look. Then shot another, with eyebrow raised, at Opal.

Opal blushed. *Message received.*

Our little band of misfits might not be stupid. But we sure were strange.

Opal sighed. "Okay. We get it, Jason. News bad. News terrible. It's just that when you talk to us like we're stupid, it takes the fun out of this cabinet thing for us. Kitchen, bathroom or otherwise."

"Don't be so sensitive, Opal! It was just a joke. Can you blame me, living with this guy?" He flicked his hand toward me.

Jason's words were met by my good buddies. Si. And Lence.

He cleared his throat and scratched his pimply Adam's apple. His eyes dropped to the agenda in his hand. "Well. Um. The news is, they're talking about closing Preston."

The sharp tang of terror filled the room.

"Good one, Waldo. I mean, Jason," I said.

"Not joking. I overheard it when I was putting some receipts into the Student Council folder in the school office. Heard Bonaparte talking to Exasperation. Sounds like the real deal. The muckety-mucks are really threatening to close down our school and merge us with Northern."

BONAPARTE
AKA NATHANIEL
(NATE) LIPSCHITZ

PRINCIPAL

ENEMY

EXASPERATION
MS. VALERIE WYCOFF
SCHOOL SECRETARY
AKA WHY COUGH?

Identifying Physical Features

• Fuzzy hair

• Cat's-eye glasses
• Squint

ENEMY

• Permanent scowl caused by repeated exposure to pickle breath

Assets: Unparalleled access to information. Sharp eyes, sharp hearing. Able to manipulate Preston staff, Parent Council members, through threats and intimidation. Controls school sign-in sheet.

Liabilities: Cranky. Hates kids and/or school.

"Are they crazy? We don't want to go to Northern! They're like—the enemy!" Lucinda said. "We hate them. Right, guys?" Her eyes darted back and forth between us for confirmation.

Opal sat back down. Crossed her legs in a yoga-y loop. "*Huh*. This does sound serious. So what's the whole story?"

"Northern has declining enrolment. They think if they shove all of us Preston kids in there, they can fill up that school. And close our building. To save money. Not to mention Preston's test scores are significantly higher than Northern's. They think they can use us Prestonians to bring up Northern's numbers and keep the State from coming down on them."

"That's so not fair!" wailed Lucinda.

My mind ticked through the day-to-day consequences of the school merger. "If we went to Northern, we'd have to go all the way across town every day, twice a day. On the bus."

"Yup—18 glorious minutes of lost freedom. Each way. I clocked it," Jason said.

"Did you now," Opal said.

"And Northern isn't just a 5 to 8 school like Preston. It's grades 5 to 12. So we'd be in there with all the high-school kids," I said.

Lucinda twisted her hands in her lap. "As if getting picked on by evil eighth-graders isn't bad enough."

"Hey—I resemble that remark," Jason said. He puffed himself up, impressed with his lame attempt at wit.

"Not you, Jason," Lucinda said with a giggle. "But you know. The Detention Gang types. I sure don't want to deal with the Wolf Lords—the older, bigger, stronger, *meaner* versions of the Detention Gang." She shuddered.

"Me neither," Opal said.

"I like Preston just the way it is!" Lucinda said. "Cozy. Comfy. Homey."

Opal coughed. A fake little cough.

"What?" I said.

"You know. Amber. She's over at Northern now."

"Uh-huh. So what does Amber say about the place, then?" Jason asked.

A squishy silence followed.

Things had gotten really tense between Opal and her twin sister earlier in the year. So tense that they'd stopped living in the same house. So tense Amber had even wound up transferring to a different school.

For Opal, the whole situation was a Very Sore Point.

I knew it. Lu knew it. Jason should have known it too.

But sometimes he was, well, such a Waldo.

I decided a speedy change of subject was in order.

I slapped my hands against my thighs and said, "So we are all in agreement, then. That a merger of Preston and Northern would be a crap idea. And we should try to prevent it from happening."

Jason nodded. "I bet my bottom dollar that the rest of Preston feels the same way."

Lucinda said, "But how can we stop it? I mean, if the school district decides it will save money."

Opal said, "And *nothing* can get in the way of improving test scores." She rolled her eyes. "They're, like, the holy grail."

Lucinda's quavery voice rose into the exosphere. "Yeah! How can we fight the holy grail?"

"That's our major, *numero uno* mission," Jason said. "Write it on your clipboard, Darren. *Missionus Toppi-Prioritius.* As your Dirk Daring alter ego would call it."

He snorfed[1] a little, and I felt my ears burn. He sure had nerve, poking fun at me even as he was begging for my help.

I was formulating a petty piece of revenge when I heard the screen door bang.

Jason and I exchanged a look. My mom wasn't due home till six. Jason's dad, not till after seven. *So who had just let themselves into our house?*

We jumped to our feet. It could be anyone, anything. It could be—

My guts went cold.

Feet pounded up the stairs. Closer, closer...

I braced myself for whatever, or whoever, was heading our way.

BAM!

The bedroom door burst open.

He stood in the opening.

Face flushed.

Eyes wild.

Travis X. Sendak.

Erstwhile best friend. One-time cohort in espionage.

---

1   TM* Word coined by Dirk Daring. Its use is legally protected by trademark. Snorf.

Now *persona non grata* with me. Sure, we had "made up" after our big blowout. We'd even run a bang-up mission together. But even so, our so-called friendship had never gone back to normal.

I didn't—couldn't—trust him anymore. Not. One. Iota.

TRAVIS X. SENDAK
AKA T-BONE

Identifying Physical Features

Pickle-shaped mole above right eyebrow

Widow's peak

Attached earlobes

Assets: IT skills. Access to enemy agents. Strategic-planning skills. Map-drawing ability

Liabilities: Untrustworthy. Consorts with enemy. Possible double agent. Untrustworthy

Previous Missions:

Status: On indefinite furlough

☆ Bug Infestation

☆ Black Ops: PA Smear Campaign

☆ Go Fish

I stepped foward and got right in Travis's face, so close I could feel his hot breath on my forehead. So close I could see the sheen of sweat on his upper lip.

Through clenched teeth, I said, "What exactly do you think you're doing, barging in here like—"

"Yeah, yeah. I know. Not welcome without a by-your-leave. But I have news. Not good news. You need to hear it."

His eyes scanned the room, taking in Opal. Lu. Jason. I could see the rise and fall of his chest. Practically hear his pounding heart.

Jason came and stood beside me, shoulder to shoulder. His solid, if lumpen, presence bolstered me.

A backward glance confirmed that Lucinda—Agent Fury—was right behind him. Opal—Agent Jewel—was in the ready position too. Her eyes shot out her patented ultra-frosty death rays.

I was glad these three were in my corner.

Jason said, "Say your piece, man. Then go."

Travis's eyes flicked from me to Jason, then back to me.

"Conner called me into his 'office.'"

Jason's pink-spotted Adam's apple bobbed up and down, up and down.

"C-C-Conner?"

"Yeah. Conner. And he wants to see you. Both of you. Now."

Into the Lair of the Beast.

I turned my collar up against the winter chill. Behind me, I heard the *snap!* of grosgrain as Agent Waldo and Agent T-Bone followed suit.

Were we walking into a trap? Very possibly. I had long been operating under the assumption that T-Bone, once my most trusted lieutenant, was a double agent. So his report was suspect. Highly suspect.

Yet Dirk Daring, Secret Agent, could not refuse an invitation from the Beast.

With my laser insight, I would see into the Beast's dark soul.

With my astute acumen, I would uncover his deepest, darkest secrets.

With utter certainty, his weakness would shine forth, in sharp relief against the black backdrop of his own foul vanity.

But exposing the Beast's vulnerability was not my only mission. I had another. It was just as crucial.

I would be assessing the T-Bone. Staking out the steak, so to speak.

Would T-Bone's true nature reveal itself too once inside the Beast's lair? Only time would tell. Time and the unerring eye of Dirk Daring, Secret Agent.

I turned my cheek and nodded to Agent Waldo. He sprinted ahead, taking up a position near the curbside mailbox.

Left, right, left, right, his head swiveled.

"All clear," he said into his collar microphone.

On cue, T-Bone stepped in front of me, taking point position.

Waldo slid into place behind me, protecting my flank.

Silently, smoothly, with our steps perfectly synchronized—left, right, left, right—we slunk toward Destiny.

Three flitting shadows briefly darkened the path to the hideout. Three flickering shadows loomed and stretched on the arched door. Three wavering shadows disappeared into the Beast's lair.

In.

Now the path took us downward. Deeper, deeper, we went, threading our way into the Heart of Darkness.

To the shores of Hades itself.

At last, we found him. It.

Ensconced in the dim, tech-twinkling, subterranean cavern he called his "room."

His hair was the color of a faded sock. His complexion, porridge dotted with currants.

But his eyes…oh, his eyes. Pure evil.

"You wanted to see us," Waldo said.

The Beast jerked his head in T-Bone's direction. "You. Go."

T-Bone glanced toward me. I nodded. He scurried from the vile chamber.

The computer lights twinkled ominously. Red LEDs flashed furiously. Humming beneath it all, I sensed the ever-present, ghostly *ermmmmmmm* of electricity.

Coursing, coursing, coursing through the veins of the labyrinthine superstructure.

The Beast's very lifeblood.

The Beast leaned back in his chair, making the wheels lose their grip on the hardwood. Making the chair's spine groan for mercy.

"It seems we have a problem," he said.

"Who do you mean, *we*?" Waldo said.

The Beast flung himself forward. His slavering jaws snapped just inches from our throats.

"Who do you think, *we*? *We* we, that's who!"

I suppressed an ignoble, indeed deadly, urge to laugh. Wee wee indeed.

The Beast flung his spidery arm in our general direction. "You, and you, have given me some serious aggro. With your round-'em-up playground stunt."

Waldo met my eye. A glimmer of a smile twisted his lip. That "stunt" a few weeks ago had gotten Preston's notorious Detention Gang off our backs and expelled from the school forever. It had been a sweet, sweet triumph. Good over Evil.

A sudden flurry of limbs, a squeaking of wheels. Waldo emitted a strangled "*Eep!*"

The Beast had him by the throat!

"Who do you think you're laughing at, you little snotnose?"

"Let him go," I murmured.

The Beast's twitchy eyes twitched in my direction. "*Ragggghht.* My little bro, Trav, tells me *you* are the mastermind of this 'operation.' That you fancy yourself some kind of 'special agent.'" He leered, revealing a glinting canine tooth. "I gotta say, you've made yourself a name, dude."

I bowed slightly. Mockingly.

"Don't get too full of yourself, kid."

He released Waldo. Then he rolled closer to me in his creepy rolly chair.

"Like I said. Because of what you did, *we* have a problem. But *we* is not going to fix it. *You* is."

He crossed his arms. Eased back in his beast-seat. Exhaled a foul waft of beast-breath.

"Cut the crap," I said. "Name your game."

He chuckled. A dark, ugly, beastified chuckle.

"My *game* is $100. A week. From now to—forever. Because my *associates*—you might know them as the Wolf Lords—"

I felt Waldo shudder.

"—are very, very unhappy that you broke up their Preston operation. It interrupted their cash flow, which I, uh, administered. And that made them unhappy with me. Which is *not* acceptable!" He swooped his hand across his black desktop, knocking speakers and keyboards and vast quantities of other blinking electronics to the floor. An errant mouse, swinging by its own cord, rubbed the table edge. It made a rubberized squeak. *Ee-erk. Ee-erk.*

Waldo gulped repeatedly.

"So you lost your seat at the Bad Boys' table," I said. "And want us to help you get it back."

The Beast's eyes widened, then narrowed to slits.

"So that's what you think, is it? Look, kid, I'm doing you a favor. My associates are only interested in maintaining their profits. Through my generous intercession, they have so far resisted breaking your heads. They've agreed to let you keep said heads by way of one simple expedient—cash."

Waldo said, "So you want us to be the Wolf Lords' new Detention Gang at Preston. Shaking down kids for their lunch money."

He shrugged his shoulders. "The Wolf Lords do not care where you find your funds. Simply that you deliver them here, every Friday, to me. A hundred dollars. No fail.

"Plus, you will add a token *service charge*. For yours truly. To compensate me for my efforts on your behalf. Shall we say, ah, 25 additional bills?"

Waldo spluttered, "One hundred and twenty-five dollars a week? Are you crazy? Who do you think we are? We don't have access to that kind of cash!"

Again, the Beast shrugged his shoulders.

"I think—no, I *know*—that you are marked men. With a price on your heads. Either you pay up, or you say goodbye to your gray matter. My associates will happily use it as whitewash for their new digs."

The Beast grimaced—or was that a smile?

He spun in his chair, showing us its back side.

"TRAVIS!" he yelled.

Agent T-Bone appeared at my elbow.

"Yeah, Conner?"

"Get these scumburgers out of our house. And remember—it's your job to collect from them. For me. You got that, Travis?"

I could smell the shame oozing from T-Bone's pores.

"Er, um. Yeah."

"And Travis?"

"Yeah, Conner?"

"Say thank you."

"What for?"

"For letting you live."

T-Bone winced.

Waldo winced.

Only Dirk Daring, Secret Agent, did not wince.

For in that moment I saw all. Knew all.

And knew exactly how I would use that knowledge to my advantage.

My Diary...
xo OPAL

January 12

Darren and I looked it up during library period last week. And this is what my spy name means in Italian!!!!! LUV IT. So I wrote this haiku. I think it doesn't suck. But maybe it does. LOL.

Allegra Montefiore

A mirthful mountain

Carpeted with flowers

Dreamland; daydreamland.

Lucinda gasped. "No!"

Jason put his fleshy palm on her shoulder. "Unfortunately, yes."

She pulled her cell phone out of her pants pocket. "I'm gonna tell my parents. This is too much for—"

Travis yanked the phone from her hand. "No you won't."

"Hey! Give that back to me!"

"Not until you promise not to tell your parents. They can't help us."

"Of course they can! They can get in touch with—somebody! Call the police!"

"*E-yuh*. As if…"

I sighed. This was *exactly* how I'd feared things would go down. Bickering and fighting, fighting and bickering. Bygones were not bygones, apparently. For any of us.

In an overly loud voice I said, "Quit it, you two. Just quit it."

Lucinda and Travis both froze.

I muscled the phone out of Travis's hand. Pried Lu's clenched fist open. Restored the phone to its former resting place and scrunched her fingers around it. With any luck, she wouldn't squeeze it so hard it smithereened.

We had enough on our plates without exploding electronics.

Opal said, "Never thought I'd say these words, but Travis is right, Lu. You know what our parents will do? Tell us to ignore the baddies. Or, worse, they'll call the high school. Make a big stink. *My little darling is being bullied, waah waah.* And you know what happens then." She raised her eyebrows and gave Lucinda a meaningful look.

Lucinda seemed to shrink before my eyes.

Yup—Lucinda knew a thing or two about being bullied. And about how much worse it got when you ran crying for mama.

Didn't we all.

Jason puffed himself up, assuming his patented I'm-the-great-poobah pose.

"The last thing you want to do is go to the cops. Then we won't have just Conner breathing down our necks. We'll have every gang member in town after us for being snitches. The cops won't be able to protect us from all of them. Not unless they can put them in a cage for life. But they can't.

"Remember—as tough as they are, the Wolf Lords are all still minors. The cops can't even hold them for more than a couple of hours. Not for stuff like this."

"How do you know that?" Travis said with a smirk. "Personal experience?"

"No, jerk. But my sister is a paralegal. She works with the courts, and with cops, all the time. She tells me stuff."

"I didn't know you had a sister!" Lucinda said. "That's totally awesome."

Opal choked back a bitter laugh. "Yeah. Right. It's the bomb. A 24/7 party."

"Half sister, actually. The bottom line is this: Tell our parents, tell the cops. Either way, we'll be toast.

You know how these things work. Pay up and shut up, or get out of town."

Jason's eyes rested for a moment on Lucinda, then moved to Opal, then to Travis and finally me. No one said boo.

"So we agree, then. We deal with this the only way we can. Head on. So we can nip this little thing in the butt."

Travis sniggered into his armpit. "I think you mean *bud*, dude."

Jason scowled. "That's what I said, Travis. Now pipe down unless you have something useful to say."

"But how can we do it?" Lucinda wailed. "I don't have any money! And I don't have any time to make any! I've got to practice!"

"When is that stupid Scrabble tournament anyway?" Opal asked sourly. "It's, like, all you ever talk about."

Lu sniffed. "Sorry. Didn't mean to bore you."

Opal's jaw tightened. "Just answer the question, okay? When's the tournament? We need to know if you'll be using it to get out of helping with"—she waved her arm around at nothing, everything—"this."

Lucinda's face turned white, then red.

Uh-oh.

She didn't get the code name Fury for nothing.

"Girls! GIRLS!" I shouted. "We're *all* a little freaked by this, uh, situation. Let's not allow it to get under our skin. Or come between us. We'll only survive this thing if we work together. So zip it!"

"Well said, little brother, well said. Don't pay any attention to her, Lu. She's a—wait—how do you spell that *B* word?" Jason blew a phony kiss at Opal.

Opal signed to him with her finger. And no, she didn't know ASL. "You. Are. So. Clever. Not," she said.

I put my head in my hands. "We're doomed," I said. "Doomed."

"Naaah," Travis said, giving me a bracing two-handed shoulder shake from behind. "Just hampered by inferior staff. That's why you need me."

I *had* needed him once. Maybe I still did.

Perhaps, more important, he needed us. Badly.

As if to confirm my thoughts, he said, "We do have to come up with some money though. Till we work out a solution. Friday is only three days away."

"Nice job on the counting," Opal said. "Maybe you could be a Scrabbler too."

Jason and Travis exchanged a look. Seems they agreed on *something*.

"So," Jason said. "Let's just ignore that juvenile outburst and focus on important things. Like ideas? For the saving of our bacon? Anyone?"

"I only know one foolproof way to make money," I said.

All eyeballs swiveled toward me.

"Ah! Yes!" Jason said. "Completely awful but also completely reliable."

"Good one," Travis said. "Why didn't I think of that!"

"Because Darren is smart and you're not?" Opal said. "That's a really good idea, D. I'm in."

"Me too," Lu said, "as long as we don't have to get our folks involved. My mom would throw a fit."

Opal said, "I'm sure we can handle it on our own. Lemme think. I bet I could get a few Odds and Ends together by…Thursday."

Jason scratched a note on a piece of paper. "Okay, so if we do it on Thursday, that gives us all of Friday to come up with any cash we're still short. In the meantime, we buy ourselves some time to figure out how to get out of this mess.

"What do you say we all go sleep on it, then? You know, let our subconsciouses work on ideas."

"Works for me, *Bud*," Travis said, getting to his feet. "But let's make this plan sooner rather than later. Okay, guys? I gotta live with Conner, you know."

Jason clapped him on the back. A bit harder than was strictly necessary. "My condolences." He turned to Lucinda. "So when *is* that Scrabble tourney?"

"My first match is two weeks from today," she said with a smile, revealing two deep dimples. I'd never noticed those before.

"Hmmm…" Jason said. "It's at Crosstown Junior School, right? Maybe I can arrange an interschool shuttle for you. To get you to your tournament in style. It's one of the perks of government office."

"You would do that? Really? For me?"

"More like the perks of being a *bud*," Travis whispered in my ear as he headed for the door.

He gave us all a jaunty wave. "Later, dudes. Glad to see everyone getting along so well."

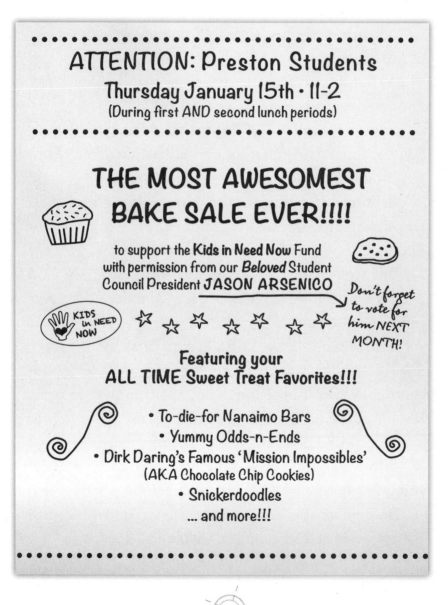

ATTENTION: Preston Students
Thursday January 15th • 11-2
(During first AND second lunch periods)

THE MOST AWESOMEST BAKE SALE EVER!!!!

to support the **Kids in Need Now** Fund
with permission from our *Beloved* Student
Council President <u>JASON ARSENICO</u>

Don't forget to vote for him NEXT MONTH!

KIDS in NEED NOW

Featuring your
ALL TIME Sweet Treat Favorites!!!

• To-die-for Nanaimo Bars
• Yummy Odds-n-Ends
• Dirk Daring's Famous 'Mission Impossibles'
(AKA Chocolate Chip Cookies)
• Snickerdoodles
... and more!!!

My Diary...
xo OPAL

January 17
9:30PM

Okay, so these so-called Kitchen Cabinet thingies really aren't that bad. Tho I can think of, like, a thousand things I'd rather do than hang out with Der Führer AND Travis X. Yuckface.

But it's kinda fun to be part of something. ~~Not just me on my own, like it's been for~~

The good news is that Waldo is not as much of a jerk as he used to be. Which is saying a lot for someone who considers himself supreme dictator of the entire school/world. I didn't believe Darren at first—leopards don't change their spots or whatever, right? But maybe he HAS learned his lesson. Like how to be a human being. (Yeah, right...)

BTW, he really does have a lot of gas (Darren's right about that 2!) He thinks nobody notices when he drops an SBD. But dude! Trust me—we notice.

Anyway, at today's meeting, the first thing we talked about was how awesome we all are, thank you thank you, for pulling together the most fantastickest bake sale ever in the history of Preston Middle School. Well, maybe not the most fantastickest ever, but it was good enough to do what we needed it to do. We earned $186 (AND 48 cents LOL)!!!!!!!!!!!!!!!

Travis took $125 of it to the Wolf Lords yesterday (or at least, he said he did). Conner told him (according to T.) that the Lords didn't really think we would do it, and they'd be disappointed they won't get to beat anybody up.

Naturally, we can't keep this up. Even if my Odds and Ends and Snickerdoodles are the best in the known universe, you can only sell (or make) so many. Dad threw a fit and a half, saying I made a mess in the kitchen and he'd only let me bake if I promised to blah, blah, blah... He's got some nerve—it's not like he's such a great housekeeper. He doesn't make a mess only because he never cooks anything.

So enuf about Dad. Back to important things, ha-ha! Today's "Cabinet" meeting.

We got together again today to come up with something better than baking like fiends every week. I do not intend to spend my life working my you-know-what off for a bunch of dead-ender gang guys. NO WAY!!!!!!!!! Needless to say, I've been wracking my brain all week trying to figure a way out of this mess. Kept coming up empty.

Don't tell anyone dear diary, ha-ha, but I'm scared that we might be in over our heads. I mean, the Preston Detention

Gang—they were kids like us. Creeps, maybe, but kids. The Wolf Lords? They're like the real deal. Some of them even have criminal records!!!!!!! They're the kind of scary dudes that wind up in jail sooner or later. I really don't want anything to do with them. But it's not up to us, is it?

I think Lu is even more freaked than me. But guess what? She's got more spunk than I knew. I woulda figured she'd head for the hills as soon as things got messy. But nope. She, it turns out, had the best idea of all of us.

Here's what she did: she offered to spy on the Wolf Lords, right on their own turf! LU!!!!!!

They hang out at Nino's Pizza. Everybody knows that. Which is one reason, dear journal, none of us Prestonians ever go there. So Lu says, "They'll never notice me. I'll just sit there, nibbling like a little invisible mouse on my pizza slice. Big mouse ears listening, listening. Maybe they'll give something away we can use. Against them." She got this real wack look in her eye when she said that.

"You'd do that?" Jason said, sounding totally shocked. "For us?"

Lu said, "Well, you can't exactly do it, Jason. They know who you are. But me?"

"As elusive, as invisible, as the unicorn of fable," Travis said. NOT in a nice way, of course.

I really, really, REALLY wanted to smack him. He is so—ugh!!! I don't care what Darren says about the jury still being out on him. I think Travis only cares about his own stupid skin.

So anyway, everybody agreed Lu would start hanging out after school at Nino's. The plan is we'll stay in texting contact.

AT ALL TIMES so if she finds herself in a jam we can swoop in and rescue her. (A job for Allegra Montefiore?!! Don't tell Dirk, but I seriously hope not... 😬)

Then Travis opens his yap and says he has an idea too. He says the Wolf Lords have their fingers in the pie over at Northern. So maybe another way to keep tabs on them is through Amber. Who he is still, apparently, all kissy-kissy with.

Naturally, this made me feel all icky and made me want to smack him even harder than before. I could feel his eyes on me, like he knew how I was feeling and was enjoying it. He is SUCH a jerk. JERKJERKJERKJERK!!!!!

Jason said, "Yeah—she could also help us with the school-merger issue. Get the story from the other side, so to speak."

I didn't say a word. Just tried to tune

them all out. La la la. I HATE talking about Amber with other people. Like she's just an ordinary girl and not ~~my own~~.

Anyway, then Darren started juggling a pencil case, a hacky sack and a superhero bobblehead thingy. Which, of course, he dropped, because he's kinda klutzy (in a kinda cute way), and he made a big goofy stink about picking everything up, which involved half-kicking Travis in the face and climbing over everyone, which drove Waldo up the wall (har-har) and made Travis look like he'd swallowed a live cockroach. I think D. did this accidentally-on-purpose as a way to change the subject. For me. Which, if it's true, would be really, really sweet.

Of course, he is still a boy, and therefore still an idiot. ☺

Stay tuned, oh journal. For the next instalment of this oh-so-gripping story.

⋀⋁⋀⋁⋀⋀⋁⋁⋀⋁⋀⋀⋁⋀⋁

Dirk Daring's Strategic Alliances Chart

TOP SECRET

ICON (name)	FIRM ALLY	Neutral/Unstable ALLIANCE	SWORN ENEMY
JEWEL	Dirk	Fury, Waldo	T-Bone, Double Trouble
FURY	Dirk, Waldo	Jewel, Double Trouble	T-Bone
WALDO		Dirk, Fury, Jewel, Double Trouble	T-Bone
T-BONE		Double Trouble, Dirk	The Beast
Bonaparte	Exasperation	Fancy Boots, Outrage, Waldo	Dirk, T-Bone
Exasperation	Bonaparte		Fancy Boots, Outrage, Waldo, Dirk, T-Bone, Fury, Jewel
Fancy Boots	Outrage		
Outrage	Fancy Boots, Double Trouble	Jewel	
Double Trouble		Jewel	

I need no disguise. I come pre-disguised. Only the purest of heart can detect me. Only the most noble, most wise.

Let's face it—there really aren't too many pure, wise, noble people out there. And pure, wise, noble types aren't hanging out in this place after school. They're doing their homework. Which is what I should be doing too. And if my mother finds out I'm not actually at the library, she is going to throw one serious fit.

But wait! I am the Unicorn. And above these petty matters.

Without further ado, I enter the humans' dining establishment.

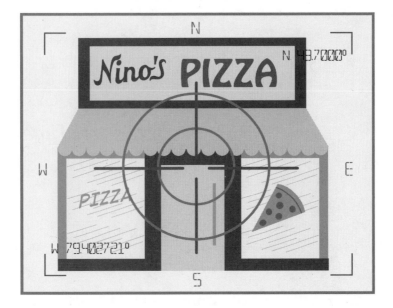

Smell the fragrance of yeast. And tomato. Is that a hint of anchovy? I hope not, because I really don't like anchovies on my pizza. I really like pizza only when it's totally plain, plain, plain.

I shake my mane, trying to free myself of these base thoughts. And remember that I am the Unicorn. I. Will. Focus.

I wait patiently to order my slice. Do not even stamp my hoof. Not once.

I cast my unicorny eye around the pizza parlor to locate my adversaries. They of the Unholy Grail.

They of the Rigged Joust. Yes—there they are—on the other side of the Plexiglas barrier between the cash-register line and the dining area. At the table by the window. A square table. Very wrong. Because if I really were a unicorn of medieval legend, it would be a round table. Like the one in the King Arthur stories. But these guys have probably never heard of King Arthur.

I'm getting kind of hungry now and want my pizza, because it smells pretty darn good.

Now I *do* stamp my hoof. I have to remind myself: I am the Unicorn. I am the Unicorn. I am the Unicorn! And unicorns are not easily distracted by petty matters. But that's not exactly true, because it's taking a really long time to get my slice. Nino, or whoever it is behind the cash—actually, I think he is named Edwin and lives down the street from me—keeps helping other people before he helps me. I guess that means my cover as the invisible unicorn remains intact, even if I'm not exactly feeling like a patient, wise, invisible unicorn right now.

I *finally* get my slice and take it to one of the stools against the window. From here I can see both the street and the Wolf Lord guys sitting kitty-corner to my left. Or maybe it's catty-corner—I never know which is right.

They don't notice me at all. Not even as a possible shakedown victim. This is definitely a good thing. Go, Unicorn!

I listen in. My unicorn horn is like an antenna, positioned to pick up everything they say.

I hear, "*Mumble mumble...guffaw.*"

Ho. Hum.

I take a bite of my pizza. It is exceedingly hot. It burns the roof of my unicorn mouth. Darn. Now I'm going to talk funny for two whole days. And it's so yucky when your mouth roof starts to peel. Stupid pizza.

"*Mumble mumble...guffaw. Mumble mumble... guffaw* Northern.*"

My unicorn ears prick up. I put down my pizza slice.

"*Mumble mumble* holy crap! Really? The basketball coach?"

Now my unicorn ears practically tingle. So does my unicorn mouth, darn it.

"This can only work in our favor," says the one that looks like a half-melted Mr. Potato Head.

"Yeah. Can anyone here spell *blackmail*?"

While they guffaw like idiots, I answer inside my own unicorn head: *Probs not...*Which is, of course, a thought unworthy of the Unicorn, but I don't care. I keep listening and nibbling until they finally free up the table and saunter toward the door.

When they are gone, I slip from my stool. Deposit my garbage in the recycling bin. And then the unicorn canters away, unseen, into the satin black of night, leaving the tantalizing scent of mozzarella in her wake.

WALDO: So you asked to see me, Principal Lipschitz?

BONAPARTE: Yes. Come in, son. Sit.

‹shuffling sound, squashing sound, squeaking sounds›

BONAPARTE: It has come to my attention that you have been up to some funny business.

WALDO: Er. Um. I don't really know what you're talking about.

BONAPARTE: Don't sass me! Or I'll have the authorities come down on you so hard you'll be begging me for mercy.

WALDO: Hey! You can't threaten a student! Besides, what authorities?

BONAPARTE: Sit back down, son. I'm not threatening you! Just calm down.

BONAPARTE: There's this little matter of, ahem, your last term's math grade...

<sound of crinkling paper>

BONAPARTE: ...and if you had received your marks honestly and fairly...or perhaps you had a little help?

<gasping sound>

WALDO: Where did you get this????

BONAPARTE: I think you know.

WALDO: But I never—I didn't—I swear!

<At this point, the sound of intense paper rustling interferes with audio quality. Rustling continues for 33.56 seconds>

BONAPARTE: Oh, really? I think you would <indecipherable> difficult to prove...if people came asking. You <indecipherable> last year's <indecipherable> answers. <indecipherable> confessed that he <indecipherable> you.

WALDO: (under breath) That little...

<paper rustling ceases>

BONAPARTE: But let's not worry about this...trifle. We have more important matters, which concern both of us, to consider.

WALDO: Are you talking about the proposed school merger?

<chair squeaking>

BONAPARTE: So you know about that, then.

WALDO: Uh-huh. I heard you and Ms. Wycoff talking about it.

BONAPARTE: Hmmm. Little dippers have big ears. ‹German expletive.› Ahem. Well, there's going to be a public meeting at the board offices in two weeks. They are going to make the proposal public then. We need to have all our ducks in a row in advance.

WALDO: What ducks are you referring to, sir?

BONAPARTE: Your ducks!

WALDO: My ducks?

BONAPARTE: Hello? Aren't you Student Council president? Of course you have ducks!

WALDO: ...

BONAPARTE: Ducks! Ducks! Your ducks! The student body!

WALDO: Preston students? I never thought of them as waterfowl, sir. If anything, they'd be pandas. Since our school mascot is a panda. ‹sound of hand slamming on desk.›

BONAPARTE: Pandas are useless. All they do is sit around and eat bamboo. It's ducks we need, and fast! Ducks to make a flap! Ducks to get down and dirty! Ducks to show the board that Preston won't go down without a fight!

WALDO: Er...sure. Ducks make so much more sense than pandas...

BONAPARTE: I'm glad you see my point. Now get quacking, or else! ‹sound of paper rustling.›

WALDO: ‹gulping sound› Yes, sir. Right away, sir.

OPAL

January 21

Two Sisters

Up

Rising, Lifting

Fly, kite, fly!

We're kissing the sky

Ecstatic in our joyful partnership

A rogue gust blows

Knocking us sideways

Falling, Crashing

Down

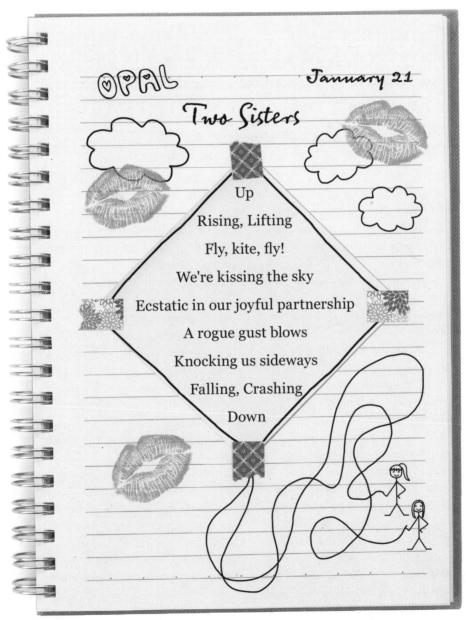

PRESTON PRESTIGE

SCHOOL MERGER THREAT!!!
Will Preston be KAPUT?

BY OPAL VEGA, STAFF REPORTER

WITH THE AIM OF CUTTING costs in Tecumseh Head School District #2, the Board of Education is considering amalgamating two schools within the district. The schools in question are Northern Senior Public School, a grades 5-12 school on the north side of town, and our very own Preston Middle School!!!!

If the merger is approved, Preston students will be bused to Northern, a trip that takes approximately 18 minutes each way. The merger would take place in September. If you are in grade 8 and wondering what will happen to you, don't worry—you will graduate from Preston in June and then go to Trevalyan High School for grades 9-12. Just like normal. Unfortunately for the rest of us, all students in grades 5-7 will go to Northern and continue there for the rest of our school careers. Which means we will all become the dreaded Northernites that we boo at during basketball games and will have to wear those ugly orange sweatshirts with the bobcat in a beret on them.

Many Preston students, naturally, are opposed to the plan. According to one grade 7 student, who has asked for anonymity, "I'm not going there. No way. That school stinks. And you are so right—the bobcat logo is totally lame. Whoever heard of a cat in a hat? Wait—that came out wrong."

Many Preston parents are also opposed. Ms. Tourmaline Vega, vice-president of the Parent Council, has children who are students at both schools. She says, "Preston and Northern are both excellent schools. But they are very different. Preston has a unique, small-school atmosphere and an excellent academic record. We shouldn't sacrifice a school as effective as Preston without careful study. Which can't be done in the few months they're talking about."

Student Council President Jason Arsenico pleased with his victory.

Jason Arsenico, Student Council president, says, "We will have a school-wide meeting next week to discuss our strategy for how to combat the merger. 'War council,' I'm calling it. I urge every Preston student to attend that meeting. We'll be assigning groups for making posters, videos and a Twitter campaign. We'll also be open to hearing your ideas on how we can stop the merger. Any ideas involving waterfowl will be given top priority."

The proposed merger will be discussed at an open meeting—for parents, students and administrators—to be held at the board office on Wednesday February 4. The proposed merger is the only item on that meeting's agenda. Students are invited to attend and make their feelings about the plan known to board officials.

If the school merger goes through, you will be wearing this hideous hoodie next fall.

Arsenico went on to say that every single Preston student should plan on going to the board meeting. "Mark it on your calendars, folks! The squeaky wheel gets the grease, and if we don't squeak loud enough, well, we'll all be meowing the Northern school song next fall."

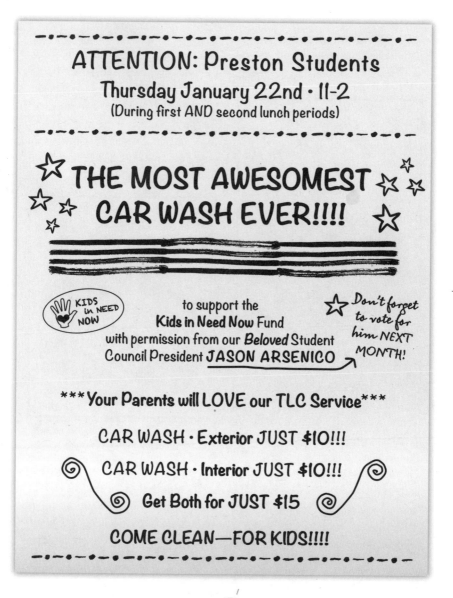

Notes from Kitchen Cabinet Meeting with Agents Jewel, Fury, Waldo, T-Bone.

06-33-44FG De-encrypted. 1/23.

"Awesome, awesome, awesome!" Opal squealed, dancing and jumping around like an idiot. "I can't believe you—*eeeeeee!*" She swung Lu around in some kind of goofy, happy-girly dance. "You are awesome! Twelve plus 50 for using all 7 letters equals 62 points worth of awesome!"

Lu was grinning ear to ear, her pink-and-purple braces shining like pink-and-purple sparklers.

"I was, like, *Omigod I'm so scared* at first, but then I just calmed down, 'cause of course they were not paying any attention to some 11-year-old girl. And then, *voilà*, they just spilled the beans."

"You were Unicorn Girl!" Opal gave Lu a high five. "Neighhhhhhh!" She clomped around in a wider circle, tossing her hair like a mane.

Lu grinned even wider. Clomped and neighed a bit too.

Definitely. Weird.

Travis gave them both a dead eye. "Are you two my-little-ponies finished with your iconic greeting ritual? 'Cause I've just about hit my sonic limit." He stuck one finger in his ear and wriggled it. "I've definitely lost several hundred hair cells on that last *squueeee* alone."

"Oh, blow it out your butt," Opal said.

"Yeah," Lu said with a titter. "Blow it."

Jason said, "But seriously, Lu, that was an awesome piece of spycraft. You got exactly what we needed. And then some."

"Agreed," I said. "I hereby give you the Dirk Daring Seal of Approval." I clapped the backs of my hands together and, yes, barked like a seal.

Travis stared at me.

Jason stared at me.

Even Lu stared at me.

But Opal giggled.

The sound made angels stop in their tracks and say, "Whoa. Nice bells."

When the magical but awkward moment passed, I said, "So how are we going to use this info? It's still pretty sketchy, isn't it? I mean, we only know that the Wolf Lords *think* there's something fishy going on with the Northern basketball coach. What that is? Not a clue."

Travis said, "Or how can we use this tidbit against the Wolf Lords? We can't exactly blackmail them for just talking about blackmailing someone else."

"True enough," Jason said. "But still. We already know the Wolf Lords have a crew that is shaking kids down at Northern, just like they did here."

"We do? How?" Lucinda asked.

"It was Amber," Travis said. "Remember? She told me."

I felt Opal tense beside me. Man, how I wished she wouldn't do that every time Amber's name was mentioned. It turned her into a ticking time bomb. One wrong move and *kerblooey*.

"So we have Wolf Lords involved in extortion at Northern. And Wolf Lords involved in blackmail, also at Northern. Put the two together and we might have something to work with," Travis said.

"Do you think Amber might already know something about this coach business?" Jason said.

Travis shrugged his shoulders. "I know she's playing basketball over there. I can ask."

Opal's body tightened up another notch. I bet she hadn't known Amber was on the team. And I bet hearing the news—from Travis, especially—was killing her.

I felt my own stomach tighten in sympathy.

"Good. Make it so," Jason said. "The more we know, the better off we will be."

"And the sooner we can make this whole nightmare go away," Lucinda said. "I can barely stand it! And yesterday! *Aargh!* My teeth are still chattering!"

"Yeah," Opal said. "The first person who says *car wash* is getting a unicorn kick right in the head." She shot a cold, hard stare at Travis.

"You said it," Lucinda said. "Whose lame idea was that anyway? As if anyone wants to get their car washed in January. Of course it was going to bomb."

"Hey! Don't look at me!" Travis said, his voice high and reedy. "You didn't have to agree to it!"

Opal said, "Oh no? What choice do we have? Either keep forking over money week after week, or your brother will—"

"Not my brother. The Wolf Lords," Travis said.

"Yes your brother. *And* his Wolf Lord pals will beat the crap out of us," Opal said. "And don't go acting all innocent on us, dude. If it wasn't for you and your twisted test-selling scheme, none of us would be in this mess!"

"I couldn't help it!" Travis squeaked. "I didn't want to. But Conner made me. Because I—"

"We know, we know, we heard all about it," Opal said with a sneer. "You broke his iPad and had to pay for a replacement. But that didn't mean you had to join the Detention Gang. Or do any of that other stuff you did."

Travis looked miserable. Opal was right—Travis *had* done some really bad things back in the fall. But he'd paid the price. And now he was trying to make things right. Not only with Conner and the Wolf Lords. But with us too. Wasn't he?

"Okay! Okay!" I said. "We've been down this road before. Travis did what he did. We did what we did. And now we move on. All right? We don't have time for the blame game.

"Travis has to bring the money back to Conner with him. Like, *now*. And we only made $40 from the car wash."

"Forty cold, miserable, wet, inadequate dollars," Opal said.

I let her comment slide. She had every right to feel bitter. We all did.

"Add that to the money we set aside last week, and we're still $23.52 short."

"We *know*, Darren," Lu said crossly.

"So let's stop chirping at each other and see if we can make up the dif. Put your cash on the table. Everybody brought their available funds, right?"

Opal threw a crinkly $10 bill onto Jason's desk. "Yup. Here's mine—the last of my Christmas money, thank you very much. I am now officially stone broke."

Lucinda sighed and dumped a handful of change next to the bill. "That's from Piggywinkle. My piggy bank."

"Oh, Lu!" Opal cried. "You didn't have to break it to open it, did you?"

Lucinda winced. "No." She shot a look of pure hatred at Travis. "It took me all night. To get the coins out of the slot. Using a nail file. And a paper clip. I would have killed someone if I had to break her. I got Piggywinkle as a birthday present when I was born. From my grandma. Who's *dead*."

Jason gave a soft whistle. "Wow. That is so…wow." He put his hand on top of hers. "Thank you. For your commitment. We will find a way to repay you."

Somehow my eyes met Travis's.

His jaw was working. His eyelids were twitching. I knew those signs—he was *this* close to losing it. Breaking out in hysterical, Waldo-inspired laughter. Rolling-on-the-floor, belly-clutching laughter.

And so was—oh no!—I!

I turned away so fast I cracked my head on the closet doorknob. So hard, it brought stars to my eyes. Which was a very good thing, because when I turned back to put my own pathetic cash offering on the pile, I had an excuse for my red face and streaming eyes.

"I got a coupla bucks. Not much. Sorry," I said. Refusing to even glance at Travis.

Jason added up the money. "Ten…12, 13, 15…and 25, 35, 45…I get $19.45. I think I can cover the rest."

"Mr. Big" pulled out his wallet. Counted out 6 dollar bills. Laid them on top of Opal's 10. And scrupulously took back 45 cents' worth of change.

"There—$125. We made it," he said.

"Just," I said. "And I don't know about you, Jason, but the rest of us are completely tapped out. Com-plete-ly."

Opal nodded. "You said it."

Lucinda sniffed. "Yup. Me and Piggywinkle both."

"Look, guys, if I had any of my own…" Travis gave us his pathetic loser look. "But you know Conner takes every penny that comes my way these days. My field-trip money. Even my lunch money."

Suddenly, everyone was looking everywhere but at Travis.

The truth was, none of us would trade places with Travis. Not for all the Piggywinkles in the world.

Jason shoved the pile of money over to Travis. "Just do it," he said.

Travis pocketed the money. He looked guilty as all get out.

"Thanks. Everyone. I swear I'll make this up to you. I don't know how yet, but I will."

"Sure. Whatever," Opal said, still not looking at him. Her finger seemed to have developed an entrancing hangnail.

I walked Travis to the front door.

On the porch he gave me one of his famous searching looks. The kind that made me feel like he could see right inside my gallbladder.

"You know I meant what I said in there, Darren. I will make this up to you."

A lump formed in my throat.

Did he mean it? Really? I thought so. I *hoped* so. But I still wasn't sure.

There was so much more to make up for than money.

I ran my hand through my hair.

Let my body sink against the doorframe.

Studied my shoes.

"Let's just deal with one thing at a time, okay?" I said.

His shoulders sank. A ragged breath escaped his lungs, and he nodded.

"Okay. I hear you. But I will, Darren. I promise."

Then Travis turned on his heel and slunk away.

ATTENTION: Preston Students
This Thursday 11-2
(During first AND second lunch periods)

THE MOST AWESOMEST
YARD SALE EVER!!!!

KIDS in NEED NOW

to support the
Kids in Need Now Fund
with permission from our *Beloved* Student
Council President JASON ARSENICO →

Don't forget to vote for him NEXT MONTH!

• Game DVDs at rock bottom prices
• FAVE movie DVDs at rock bottomer prices
• Vintage clothes boutique —a shop-n-swap extravaganza!!!!
• and more!!!

Go the EXTRA Distance—A Yard, Perhaps?—For Kids!

Waldo stuck his head into my room.

"Can we talk?"

I looked around in confusion. Was he talking to me? On purpose? Something had apparently caused the universe to wobble on its axis.

"Sure…" I said with a degree of unease.

The last time Waldo had wanted to chat with me one-on-one, it was because he had decided to use my stolen spy journal as a tool of extortion. I could only imagine what he had up his sleeve this time.

Waldo sat down on the edge of my bed. He let his hands fall between his knees. His head dropped too.

He mumbled something unintelligible.

"Excuse me?"

He cleared his throat. Mumbled again: "I need to ask you a favor."

I leaned back against my pillow.

Now this was interesting…

"Shoot," I said.

"I need you to break into Bonaparte's office."

I sat bolt upright.

"What? Are you crazy?"

"No crazier than you, dude. You've sneaked into the school office before. I'm just asking you to—"

"To do a little freelance breaking and entering. Not into the school office, which is a piece of cake. But the *principal's* office. Which is illegal. Not to mention kind of dangerous."

"I know. And I wouldn't ask you if it weren't important."

I raised one eyebrow. "It would have to be."

"Bonaparte's got something of mine. If I don't get it back, I could be in deep doo-doo."

I wracked my brain trying to imagine the possibilities.

Waldo looked so dejected, defeated, I thought he might cry.

"Spill it, Jason."

He groaned. "Let's just say we have a serious math problem."

Understanding dawned. It was math tests—old ones that Waldo had bought but never used—that had caused us all so much trouble last fall. We all thought we'd buried that body.

But now, it seemed, Bonaparte had uncovered the corpse.

And he had evidence. Hard evidence.

If so, Waldo's glory days as Student Council president were numbered. He could even be expelled.

Waldo's future lay pulsing in the palm of my hand.

"How'd he get the evidence?" I asked.

"I have no idea! I just know that I'm a dead man if I don't get it back."

"Bonaparte's office is always locked. Unless he's in it, or Ms. Wycoff is guarding it. Not exactly the easiest of missions you're asking of me, Jason."

"You can do it, Darren. I know you can." He gave me the pleading puppy eyes. So pathetically earnest I could practically hear them woof.

"And if I do?"

"You'll be saving my bacon, bro. Hugely. And I'll owe you huge back."

Owing me huge...I certainly liked the sound of that.

"Let me think about it," I said.

Jason lumbered to his feet. "Will you? For real? You know I wouldn't drag you into this if it weren't—"

"I said I will, so I will, okay? Now get out of here. I've got homework."

I showed him my textbook—*Patterns in Mathematics.* A coincidence, I swear.

Jason gave me a wry smile. "Thanks, dude." Then he was gone.

He slunk back to his own room. The bedsprings squeaked and groaned as he flung himself into his favorite position, the sprawled lobster.

Did I actually hear a stifled sob?

A twinge of pity flared in my heart. He was my brother, after all, even if only of the step kind.

And we had turned a new leaf since autumn, hadn't we?

Besides, no problem, math or otherwise, was too difficult to solve. Not for Dirk Daring, Secret Agent.

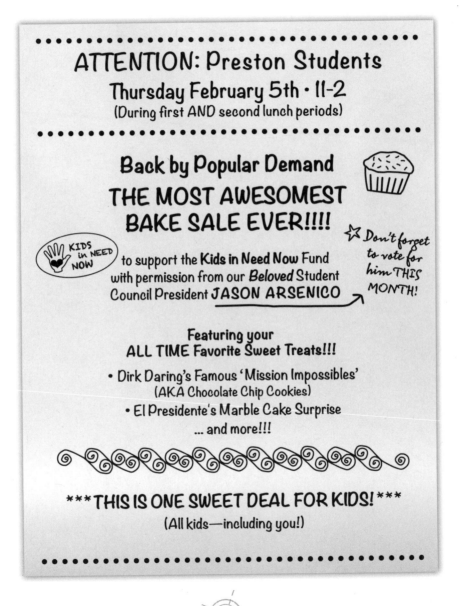

ATTENTION: Preston Students

Thursday February 5th · 11-2

(During first AND second lunch periods)

Back by Popular Demand

THE MOST AWESOMEST BAKE SALE EVER!!!!

KIDS in NEED NOW

to support the **Kids in Need Now** Fund with permission from our *Beloved* Student Council President **JASON ARSENICO**

☆ *Don't forget to vote for him THIS MONTH!*

Featuring your ALL TIME Favorite Sweet Treats!!!

• Dirk Daring's Famous 'Mission Impossibles'
(AKA Chocolate Chip Cookies)
• El Presidente's Marble Cake Surprise
... and more!!!

THIS IS ONE SWEET DEAL FOR KIDS!

(All kids—including you!)

12:22 PM. PA Announcement

ATTENTION!
ATTENTION PRESTON STUDENTS.

The fire alarm has been triggered in the south corridor. Will all students please proceed to the nearest exit immediately.

To Repeat: *The school fire alarm has been triggered in the south corridor. Will all students please proceed to the nearest exit immediately.*

Where There's Smoke, There's Fire.

The noise is deafening.

A trilling, beeping, howling cacophony.

The smoke is choking.

A gagging, swirling, panicky thickness.

Chaos, naturally, ensues.

But Dirk Daring, Secret Agent, does not succumb. He is the calm, still eye at the center of the storm.

Mere danger does not, cannot, impede my mission.

It propels me.

I am, in fact, all fired up.

I head into the choke of smoke. Relying on my keen sense of direction, I slip from alcove to alcove, recess to recess.

Remember that nothing less than the fate of the nation is at stake.

I dart. Dart again.

Luck is with me. I remain unseen as I make my way upstream. To the inner sanctum. The Principality of Bonaparte.

HISSS...

I turn the knob.

CRRRK...

The door opens. I am inside!

But, like Russian dolls, the enemy's HQ is nested. A room. Within a room. Within a room.

First the outer office. Then the inner office. And only then...

I retrieve my toolkit from my secret pocket. Within it, a device for jimmying a door, disguised as an ordinary library card.

Perfect for an object designed to obtain information.

I slide the stiff plastic between door and frame. Use my finely honed tactile sense to jiggle it just so.

CLICK...

The lock on Bonaparte's door surrenders to my ministrations.

I turn the knob.

CRRRK…

In!

I check my stopwatch—3 minutes, 49 seconds has elapsed.

An eternity.

I yank open desk drawers. Left, right. Left, right. Searching with my photographic memory for the target image.

Elapsed time—6 minutes, 23 seconds.

Nothing.

I pivot on my heel, searching, searching for a clue. I spy, with my little eye…

It falls upon the file cabinets.

I storm the barricade of metal. Paw through the endless rows of drawers. One. By one. By one.

Nothing. Just the smell of smoke, thick in my nostrils. The scent of evil, ripe in my nose.

Elapsed time—10 minutes, 2 seconds.

Too long.

The bell rings. *The all clear!*

Again—cacophony. Trilling. Beeping. Howling.

I fight against distraction, drawing upon my

considerable strength of will. Am I not Dirk Daring, Secret Agent? Incorruptible, undistractable?

As I collect myself, my eye falls upon a daypack.

Brown.

Frayed.

Stuffed casually under the desk.

I seize the daypack.

Rifle through it.

And—retrieve?

Math Test

1. Find the difference between the following polynomials
A) $6x^2-5x+2$ and $-8x^2+7x-1$
B) $-8q^2+4$ and $-q-6$

2. Simplify

Math Test

1. Find the difference between the following polynomials
A) $6x^2-5x+2$ and $-8x^2+7x-1$
B) $-8q^2+4$ and $-q-6$

2. Simplify
A) $16x^2$

4. The number of days left in the month of September are one fifth of the number of days already passed. How many are left in the month?

number of days left in the month of September are one fifth of the number of days already passed. How many days are left in the month?

MATCH MATCH MATCH!!!

Reprieve!

With utmost care, I slip from Bonaparte's (*HISSSSSS*) secret sanctum.

Slip from the inner office.

Slip from the outer office.

Into the slipstream of returning students.

When all is clear, I slip the incriminating document into the pocket of the President.

He rewards me with a curt nod.

It is enough, more than enough, for Dirk Daring, Secret Agent.

Because thanks to me, the Government is safe. For now.

WALDO: So you asked to see me, Principal Lipschitz?

BONAPARTE: Yes. Come in, son. Sit.

‹shuffling sound, squashing sound, squeaking sounds›

BONAPARTE: So. ‹sound of pencil tapping on desk› Are all your ducks in a row?

WALDO: No, sir. I do not have any ducks.

BONAPARTE: I thought we had a deal.

WALDO: Not exactly. I mean, I want the school merger to be stopped just as much as you do, sir. But I haven't a clue how to do that. I'm just a student. I think that's your job, sir. Since you're the principal here.

BONAPARTE: Get that smug smirk off your face! Have you

forgotten about this? ‹shuffling sound, squashing sound, squeaking sounds› ‹expletive: deleted› **Wait!** ‹expletive: deleted› **Where'd it go?** ‹German expletive: deleted›

WALDO: I think you will find you no longer have any power to intimidate me, sir.

BONAPARTE: Why you little...When—how did you get in here? I oughta...

WALDO: I also think, Mr. Lipschitz, you'd better get cracking on your speech for the board-wide meeting tomorrow night. To, um, explain your failure to maintain order in the school...

BONAPARTE: Speech! ‹gulping sounds›

WALDO: ...and save Preston. But we're both on the same side on this, aren't we? As you so definitely pointed out.

‹sound of a rubber duck squeaking›

BONAPARTE: ‹mumbling› Speech? ‹indecipherable› Valerie always writes my ‹indecipherable› speeches. And she's out with the ‹expletive: deleted› shingles...No way can I make a speech...

WALDO: Oh really? Perhaps, then, I can help you. And all my little ducky friends too...

‹sound of duck squeaking›

And at some future date, maybe you can ‹indecipherable› the favor...

‹sounds of knuckle-cracking, chuckling. Swearing (German)›

Notes from Board-Wide Meeting to Discuss Possible School Merger.

HNB6432121XYOLA!1 De-encrypted. 2/4.

You know how books sometimes say, *The tension was so thick you could cut it with a knife*? I always thought that was ridiculous. You can cut bread with a knife. You can cut steak with a knife. But tension? Gimme a break.

That was before tonight's board meeting.

Now I get it.

The tension was so thick you could even smell it. A tangy, musky brew of yuck.

I waved my hand under my nose. "So this is why they always serve coffee," I said to Opal. "To cover the stench of pissed-off grown-up."

She giggled. "The reek of rage."

"And Outrage," I said slyly.

OUTRAGE
(TOURMALINE VEGA)

(Parent Council Vice-President)

Known associates: Amber and
Opal Vega (daughters)

Identifying Physical Features

Big hair

Bedazzled

"Hey. That's my mom you're talking about. Don't get smart with me."

"Just yanking your chain. You know I didn't mean anything."

"Yeah. I know." Opal punched me lightly on the bicep. "You don't."

My stomach twisted.

"Yah! Gotcha. Uh-oh. Look!"

My heart was pounding crazily in my ears. *What did she mean, I didn't mean anything? Did she mean not to her? Or did she mean she—*

"Darren! Snap out of it! We've gotta get over there right now!"

I looked. Outrage—Ms. Vega—was toe-to-toe with Fancy Boots. Co-chair of the Preston Parent Council. And Outrage's bestie.

FANCY BOOTS
(TRACEY PAISLEY)

(Parent Council President)

Identifying Physical Features

• Smirk of superiority

• Expensive highlights

Or rather, judging by the matched expressions of anger on their faces, her extie.

We hurried up to them. Fancy Boots was talking down to Outrage like she was lady of the manor and Outrage was the serf.

"It's so obvious, Tourmaline, that the merger is a good idea. They have a gifted program at North—"

"Oh, so *that's* it. You're in favor 'cause you think Callie will get into it? Even though she didn't score high enough on the gift—"

"How dare you talk about my daughter!"

"How dare you think you can push your way—"

"Mom!" Opal rushed in and threw her arms around her mother. "I feel like I haven't seen you in ages!"

Ms. Vega squeezed Opal back. She kept glaring, though, over the top of Opal's head, at Fancy Boots.

"My sweetie!" Ms. V. gave Opal a big kiss. "How's my girl. Everything okay over at Daddy's?"

"*Humph.*" Fancy Boots sniffed. "You have no business getting involved in school policy. Seeing that you can't even keep your own family together."

Ms. Vega reared up like a pissed-off rhino.

"HOW DARE YOU! YOU—YOU—"

"MOM!" Opal physically dragged her mother away from Fancy Boots. "You know Darren, right?"

I knew I had to step up. Keep this thing from spinning out of control. So I swallowed hard, stuck my hand out like a grown-up and said, "Darren Dirkowitz. I think you know my mom from Aquafit."

Outrage blinked a few times. Pulling herself together, I could tell.

"Why yes! Of course! Nice to meet you!" she said. Then Opal took over, chattering with her mom about God knows what.

I'll admit it—I was rattled. If Fancy Boots and Outrage were at each other's throats, this was gonna be one helluva meeting.

That's when Jason appeared. Bustling in all "on top of it," all focus and resolve and pompous twit-ness.

Exactly what the moment called for.

Jason thrust himself between Opal and Ms. V.

"Ms. Vega? I'm Jason Arsenico. Student Council president."

"Darren's stepbrother," Opal said.

"Right. Of course," Ms. V. said.

Jason tapped his clipboard. "I've got the meeting agenda right here. For when the pro-Preston side gets our turn. We've set it up so you speak first. Then the

Preston Spirit Club is going to do a pep number. And then Bonaparte—er, Principal Lipschitz—is going to take the mic. You okay with that, Ms. Vega?"

"Uh-huh," she said, cutting a dark look over at Fancy Boots. "Can. Not. Wait."

"Good." He turned to us. "Now, when Bonaparte gets up to the stage, that's where you guys come in. You on it?"

"On it," I said.

"My crew is ready too," Opal said. "But I'm not sure about Lu. Anyone seen her?"

A voice behind me made me jump.

"She's over there. With her squad."

It was Travis.

And he wasn't alone.

Opal froze.

Amber froze.

"Hey," Opal said.

"Yeah," Amber said. "Come on, Trav. There's someone I've got to talk to." She took his hand and started off.

Opal grabbed Amber's shoulder and spun her around. "Don't you do that!"

"Let go of me!"

"Don't you dare do that! Pretend you don't see me! Pretend you don't know me! I'm your sister! You can't wish me out of existence!"

"You see?" Fancy Boots sniffed at Outrage. "Your own children can't get along."

"Tracey Paisley! Did those words just come out of your mouth? Because if they did, you are gonna lose some of those expensive teeth, girl…"

"Let go of me, Opal. You're hurting me," Amber said through clenched teeth.

"Well, you're hurting me!" Opal cried. Her face twisted in on itself. She made a raspy, strangled sound, then flung herself away from Amber and disappeared into the crowd.

"Opal!" I shouted after her. But she was gone.

I turned back to Amber, ready to give her a piece of my mind. But she was knuckling her eyes. Her chest was heaving.

Travis was rubbing her back. Whispering into her ear. He caught me watching and gave me such a long, dark, strange look that I thought I just might throw up.

I didn't know what to do. To my left, Ms. V. and Fancy Boots were still locked in their own private battle. To my right, Travis and Amber.

And there I was, in the middle. Alone.

Like I said, you could cut the tension with a knife.

Notes from Board-Wide Meeting to Discuss Possible School Merger.

2-HNB6432121XYOLA!2 De-encrypted. Part II. 2/4.

At one point or another, the board meeting was called to order. I had no idea who the first speakers were or what they said. I was too busy hunting for Opal. But she wasn't anywhere in the auditorium. I figured she was hiding in the ladies' room.

I was plotting how to get into it without getting my butt kicked by somebody's mother when the whole room erupted in noise.

Preston kids.

They were booing.

I craned my neck to see what was going on.

Fancy Boots had taken the stage.

Every time she tried to speak, the noise level swelled.

Wolf whistles.

Clanging noisemakers.

Chants of "NO! NO! NO! WE! WON'T! GO!"

Out of the corner of my eye, I saw Ms. Paisley's daughter bolt from the auditorium.

The chants, the wolf whistles, the clangs and clacks and boo-yas just kept on and on.

Eventually, Fancy Boots gave up and sat down. Her face? Well, let's just say for once in her life she didn't look all Miss Pretty. She looked like a vicious, molting hyena.

Next, Opal's mother took the stage. Again, the auditorium erupted. But this time the interruptions were cheers.

War whoops.

Tooting horns.

Chants of "Preston! Preston! Preston!"

At the end of her speech, the Spirit Club jumped in to do its bit. There were more cheers and a song about how fabulous Preston was blah, blah, blah.

Then the board chair invited Bonaparte to the stage.

That was my cue.

I checked my pockets. Good to go.

I double-checked my crew. They all gave me a thumbs-up.

I sent my own thumbs-up to Jason. He turned his head to the right. I could see Lu sending her *ready* signal back to him. Travis too. Opal, though, was nowhere to be seen.

"*Ahem*," Principal Lipschitz—Bonaparte the Bone-head—said into the mic. "Is this thing on?"

A collective groan rose from the audience.

"Okay. Yes. Well, then. Best get started. In my—*ahem*—tenure as principal at Preston—"

At the word *Preston*, we sprang into action.

All of us Preston kids ripped off our shirts to reveal bright yellow T-shirts underneath. They were emblazoned on the front with the words *PRESTON DUCK SQUAD*. On the back, the shirts read, *We won't quack under pressure!*

We tossed gobs of confetti into the air, most of it duckling-yellow. Duck-like kazoo blats rent the air.

Travis shouted, "Three quacks for Principal Lipschitz! The best principal in the world! Hip hip—"

"Hooray!" came the response from the Prestonians.

"Hip hip—"

"Hooray!"

By the third "hip hip," we were at the stage, muscling our Fearless Leader away from the mic and onto a chair. 5—6—no, 20 of us—then proceeded to carry him around the auditorium, shouting, "Lipschitz, Lipschitz, Lipschitz!"

Lu's crew, meanwhile, had unrolled a giant yellow banner that read, *SAVE PRESTON!* They marched with it across the stage. Matching yellow signs—in the shape of ducks, of course—popped up in the audience. They bobbed up and down in time with the chant.

And then Jason was on the stage, his voice booming over the loudspeaker. "Look at that! The feeling we Preston students have runs true and runs deep. We know we are blessed at our school. Thanks to our awesome principal, Nathaniel Lipschitz! He has made our school beloved by generations of Preston students!"

Bonaparte looked stunned, but he smiled and nodded. Smiled and nodded. Bonaparte the Bobblehead.

"If Preston is closed, we will all suffer. No way will we succeed the way we succeed now, under Principal Lipschitz's guidance! Look at our state test scores!

Number six in the whole state! You'd have to be cracked—no, quacked!—to mess with success like that!"

A barrage of very ducky kazoo blats filled the air.

Jason shouted, "Let's hear from the people. What do you want, people?"

"SAVE PRESTON!" The room shook with the sound of 300, maybe 400 people shouting.

"When do you want it?"

"NOW!"

Jason kept it up—call and response, call and response—until our voices were hoarse, our ears rang, and 5—10—no, 20 people's arms shook with fatigue. We put Bonaparte down fast.

Finally, the board chair wrestled the mic away from Jason. "Speaking on behalf of my fellow members, we are grateful for your, um, enthusiastic expression of feeling here tonight. I think we can safely say—yes? Yes, we can say that this matter will be put on hold. Pending, er, further consultation with parent groups and other stakeholders."

A huge cheer, and a smattering of quacks, rose from the floor.

"The meeting is now over. Please, everybody, go home. And drive safely. Thank you."

It was a thrilling moment. A perfect moment—if only Opal had been there with me.

I had to go find her.

I pushed my way through the milling crowd, heading toward the washrooms. Past the unattended coffee-and-donuts sale table.

Travis ran up to me. His face was flushed, his eyes bright.

"Looks like we did it, huh?"

"Yeah. Cool."

"What's wrong?"

"Opal. I can't find her. I'm worried about her."

His brow knit.

"Yeah. That was pretty unpleasant. Want me to help you look for her?"

"Thanks, but no thanks. I don't think she'd be too happy to see you right now."

"No. I guess not..."

"So? You and Amber?"

"Naah. Just...you know. Friends." He gave me a wink. "For now."

He shot me a V-sign and sauntered off.
That's when I saw it.
His pockets. They were bulging.
With cash.

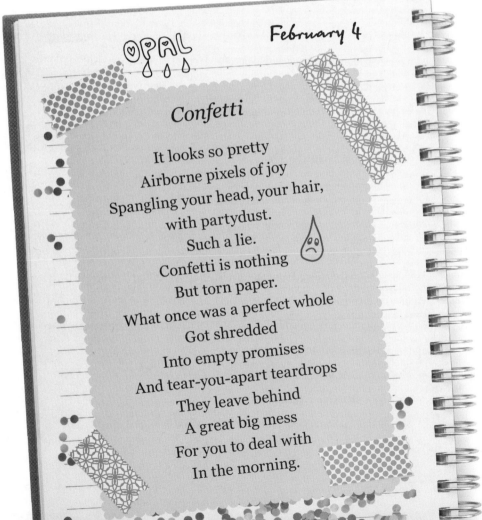

OPAL

February 4

Confetti

It looks so pretty
Airborne pixels of joy
Spangling your head, your hair,
with partydust.
Such a lie.
Confetti is nothing
But torn paper.
What once was a perfect whole
Got shredded
Into empty promises
And tear-you-apart teardrops
They leave behind
A great big mess
For you to deal with
In the morning.

Jason hammered on his desk with his fist. "Settle down, people! We have lots to sort out here. And not much time!"

Lucinda's forehead crinkled. "But we made enough money from today's bake sale! Didn't we? Your marble cake was really, really good, Jason."

"Thanks. And yeah, we did. It's not about that. Ms. Paisley sent me a text. She said the money the Student Council made from coffee sales last night was stolen!"

"Oh god," Opal groaned, shaking her head.

"And that money was going to be used to buy new books for the school library."

"Which we definitely need," Lucinda said, nodding so vigorously I thought the Hello Kitty barrettes might fly right out of her hair.

Opal asked, "So are you saying the Detention Gang is back to its old tricks?"

"How can they be? All those guys were expelled!" Lucinda squealed.

I shot a look at Travis. He was studiously picking at a jam stain on his knee. Raspberry, it looked like.

Jason shrugged. "You don't think the Wolf Lords have been busy recruiting new blood? A new Detention Gang?"

I cleared my throat. "It doesn't have to be a Detention Gang kind of thing. Anyone could swipe money. A kid. A grown-up…anyone."

"Isn't that right, Travis?"

His body jerked like he'd been shocked.

He gaped at me.

I nodded at him. *Yes, I know. I saw you,* my eyes said. And: *You let me down. Again.*

Opal closed her eyes. "Tell me you didn't steal the coffee money, Travis."

Travis's shoulders collapsed. "I took the money," he mumbled into his lap.

"WHAT THE—!" Jason shouted, slamming his fist over and over on the desk. "You don't think we have enough problems without you going and stealing from Student Council? I oughta—"

"I did it for us, okay?" Travis said. "So we wouldn't get caught short again, like last week. So you guys didn't have to cough up any more cash. So I could contribute something too. Since this whole freaking mess-up is my fault."

He reached for his backpack. Rustled around inside it. And then withdrew a wad of cash and a ziplock bag filled with coins.

Travis tossed the money into my lap.

"Here it is. Every penny."

Opal shook her head. And shook it. And shook it. "You are *such* a—"

"You're right. I am. I wasn't thinking, okay? I just saw the open cash box and all that money just sitting there. No one was watching it, and I just thought it could help. Us."

"*You*," Opal spat.

"*Us*," Travis insisted. "And now I realize it was stupid—"

"Colossally stupid, dude," Jason said. "Not to mention illegal."

"Yeah," Travis said. "Look. You're right. I'm a jerk and I make really, really bad decisions. I don't blame you for hating me. But I was doing this to help you guys out. Trust me, I can't even sleep worrying about this."

Misery and desperation wafted off him like smoke from a weenie roast.

He fidgeted. Fidgeted some more. Then he got to his feet.

"But now I know what I have to do. I'm going to call the police. I'll tell them what's going on, that it's all my fault, and get them to stop this whole nightmare. The Wolf Lords will leave you alone. They'll just come after me."

"Sit back DOWN!" Jason boomed. "You are *not* going to do that."

"No. You're not," I said.

"Why not?" Lu said. "He deserves whatever he gets. Stealing money and whatever else." She shot him a look so cold it could freeze lava in its tracks.

"He's not going to do that because 1, it won't work. And 2, he's telling the truth," I said. "He did a bad thing, but he did it for the right reasons. Which makes it only a half-bad thing in my book."

Travis looked at me. A sad shadow of a smile crossed his lips. "Thanks, D."

"Doesn't mean you are forgiven," I said, my voice sounding sharp even to my own ears. "Or that we still don't have a problem. Because now we have to get this money back to the Student Council."

"I'll do it." Travis put his hand out for the money.

I held it farther away from him. "Without being caught."

"I think that makes it another job for Dirk Daring," Jason said. Giving me a wide grin.

"So Darren gets the money back to Ms. Paisley somehow. That still doesn't solve our bigger problem," Opal said.

"Yeah. That we can't keep feeding the Beast," Lu said.

"Agreed," Jason said. "But anyone have any long-term answer? Other than stealing other people's money?" When no one answered, he sighed and said, "I thought not. So until we do, we're gonna have to keep doing these fundraisers."

A collective groan rose.

"Now, now, dweebies! Don't go all despairy on me! We have plenty of options! For example, guess what's coming up in just over a week?"

Lucinda brightened. "Valentine's Day!"

"Uh-huh. And what a perfect fundraising opportunity that lovely arrow-shooting, pink-wearing, Red Hot-eating celebration of love offers us. Who doesn't need Valentine's Day gifts?"

"And cards! And treats!" Lucinda bounced a little. "I adore Valentine's Day. Don't you?" She looked expectantly at each of us.

Opal looked green. Travis, white. And me? Well, let's just say I wasn't feeling in the pink either.

Jason, on the other hand, beamed. "I knew I could count on you, Lu, to share the Valentine's spirit! So I called my sister, Karen. She works part-time at Sheridan Nursery. And she's gonna get us some cute little cycla-whatevers—those plants with the droopy hot-pink flowers—at less than wholesale. We can sell them at a huge profit."

Lu chimed in. "We have heart-shaped cookie cutters I can use to make supercute cookies! Will you help me, O.? We can ice them in pink with red sparkles and put messages on them, like on those candy hearts. You know, things like 'Too cute' and 'Preciousssss.'"

Opal smiled. A smile, I noticed, that didn't reach her eyes. "Sure."

Jason said, "I thought we could also take videos of people asking other people to be their valentine. They can send 'em from their phones. We could charge a buck a pop—100 percent profit."

I sneaked a peek at Travis. Still sitting with his hands in his lap. Looking awful.

I didn't think he'd be getting any valentines this year.

I sneaked a glance at Opal too. She didn't look much better than Travis.

Travis was on his own. But Opal was a different matter.

I decided there and then to make sure she got a valentine this year. From someone special. Someone who really, really cared about her. Down deep.

Even if—gulp—it killed me.

Deflection.

Every mission is different.

No matter how many times one walks the same route, the path is different.

This mission, no different.

I don my cloak—one of mystery.

My co-agent dons her cloak—one of misinformation.

I slip back into the school.

She slips into the student body.

Discreetly, silently, I make my way to the office.

Loudly, indelicately, she spreads the story.

CRRRK. CRRRK.

Did you hear? Did you hear?

SHUFFLE. SHUFFLE.

*It was the new kid! Yeah! The new kid! You know—
the tall, pale guy? You've seen him! Everyone's seen him! A
transfer from Northern!*

SCReeK! SCReeK!

*He scooped up the Student Council cash! Because it
was sitting unattended, and he was afraid it would be
stolen!*

I pull the package from my pocket. The ziplock bag
full of money. And the note.

To Whom It May Concern:

Here is the money from the board meeting coffee
table. I saw it unattended. I thought someone might,
steal it. So I took it to keep it safe. Sorry I didn't
let you know sooner.

Signed

An Anonymous Preston Student

The new kid is a Hero!
The new kid is a Hero!
The new kid is a Hero!
I slip from the office.
Slip off my disguise.

And return to the Real World. Where I exchange fist bumps with my colleague.

To celebrate that no one truly knows the shadowy doing of Dirk Daring, Secret Agent.

To celebrate that no one truly knows the shadowy doings of Allegra Montefiore, Secret Agent.

And to celebrate the nonexistent new kid, the "hero" of the day.

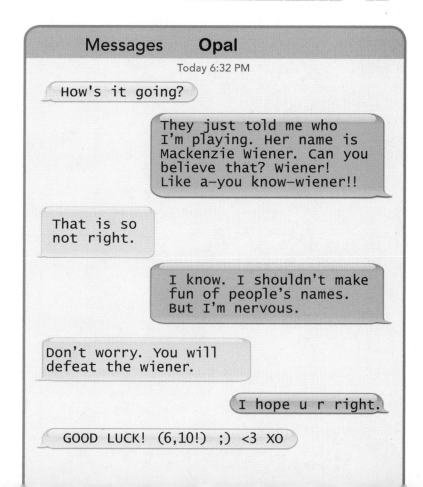

Messages **Opal**

Today 6:32 PM

How's it going?

They just told me who I'm playing. Her name is Mackenzie Wiener. Can you believe that? Wiener! Like a—you know—wiener!!

That is so not right.

I know. I shouldn't make fun of people's names. But I'm nervous.

Don't worry. You will defeat the wiener.

I hope u r right.

GOOD LUCK! (6,10!) ;) <3 XO

Mission 12BMX

Case Report 45h678373604c58h38kp0

De-encrypted. 2/12. Via Agent Fury.

Consorting with the Enemy.

So I'm a little nervous about this mission. I don't think my unicorn disguise is going to work, but Darren (oops! I mean Dirk) says I should just keep my lip zipped and everything will work out fine.

I've never been to Northern before, and, okay, it looks a lot like a jail. High beige walls and these weird, narrow windows like arrow slits. And I think, *Please please please I don't want to go in there. Please please please don't let them merge Preston until after I grad-uate.* But Dirk just walks on ahead like he's been here a million times before. He says he hasn't, but he's being all

Dirk Daring-y and it's like he's another person. Totally confident—so much so that it's a little scary.

I canter to keep up with him—I *am* the Unicorn LOL!—and he shows me a map of the school. I ask him where he got it, and he just gives me this dark look like, *You are such a derp.* So I clam right up and let him show me where the entrance usually propped open by the kids is, and where the coach's office is.

We "synchronize our watches," which is kind of silly because they are not actually watches—they are phones. And phones always have the right time because they are synchronized with a satellite somewhere, so of course our phones already match. But I don't say anything about that. Zip.

We wait for the bell to ring. Northern's schedule is, like, 25 minutes behind ours—something to do with the bus schedule—so we were able to get out of school and bike over (er, canter over—a unicorn never reveals her true methods of transportation) before their classes let out.

Then it rings, and the whole school empties out except for the after-school clubs, sports teams and kids in detention.

We make our way through the crowd, and we are invisible. Me, because I am the magical unicorn of myth with my own invisibility spell, and Darren—Dirk—because he is the world's best secret agent and can just disappear, even when you are looking *right at him*. When he wants to disappear, I mean. Not just because he's a nobody.

We go to the door that has a wedge of wood to keep it from slamming totally shut. But it doesn't matter, because kids are still coming out, so the door is wide open. And just like that, we are inside the enemy citadel.

It takes a few seconds for my eyes to adjust to the light, but my oh-so-sensitive unicorn nose notices immediately that Northern smells exactly like Preston. A mixture of paste, stinky shoes, paper and old tuna. But it's much bigger then Preston—the hallway is dark and seems to stretch on forever, with ugly flesh-colored lockers lining both sides. I wonder who decorated this place and if they were, like, totally color-blind. Then again, not everyone has the acute sensitivity of a unicorn.

The corridor is pretty well empty, so Dirk walks straight down the middle like he belongs here and knows exactly where he is going. He doesn't look left, right or anything—I do, because I am dead curious. But there's nothing to see, nothing to fear. Unless you get the willies when ten giant guys in bright orange football uniforms come barrelling down a side corridor right toward you.

Dirk doesn't change his pace. He doesn't alter his stone-cold rhythm, and I follow him down a hallway even stinkier than the last one. I realize we are right beside the school gym, and then, right in front of us, is our elusive destination. The coach's office.

"Now what?" I whisper.

"We wait," Dirk says in an undertone. "Our rendez-vous will take place in exactly 3.5 minutes."

I read the posters stuck up on the bulletin board, advertising sign-ups for cheerleading tryouts. I start getting antsy because I don't know if this is going to work. And my mom is going to kill me if I'm not home right on time, or if I don't get my homework done before Jazz Dance class tonight. Because, as she reminds me every week, it's costing a fortune on top of all the other lessons and school supplies, et cetera et cetera.

Our contact materializes.

She eyes us suspiciously.

"Travis said you wanted to see me."

Dirk nods. I nod.

Double Trouble (AKA Amber) crosses her arms.

"Make it fast."

Dirk pulls her close to him. Whispers in her ear.

I observe her. See a series of expressions cross her face. Doubt. Surprise. Interest. Annoyance.

She is as easy to read as a child's fairy tale. Grimm, LOL.

She puts out her hand.

Dirk slips something into it.

Her fingers close over it.

"Okay. I'll do it. For Travis, since he asked me. And for Northern, okay? Not for you. Just so we got that straight."

Dirk jerked his chin. "We have the same enemy. That makes us friends."

She laughed, a loud, horsey Double Trouble laugh. "Don't bet on it."

"One more thing," he said, pulling her even closer. He whispered in her ear. So softly that even my sensitive unicorn ears couldn't make the words out.

"Sure thing. Right," Amber, I mean Double Trouble, said and laughed again—or was that a snort? "I'll def be doing that."

Then she turned to me. "Oh hi, Lucinda. Didn't see you standing there." She brayed her ugly mule laugh one more time. Ugh. "Give Trav a kiss for me, okay?"

If I were not the Unicorn, a truly noble beast gifted with self-control and wisdom, I would have thrown myself upon Her Mulishness and ripped her face off. But I *am* the Unicorn. Above petty human rivalries, petty human jealousies. Above equine jealousies too.

At least, that's what I kept telling myself as I tromped along beside Dirk back to our bicycles.

"I can't believe I let you talk me into this. You can't trust that creature. She is so going to blow it," I said.

"No she won't," Dirk said, but his tone belied his words. His famous Dirk Daring confidence was gone.

In fact, he sounded…sad?

Which left me wondering what that secret whisper was really all about. Because it sure didn't seem to have anything to do with the Detention Gang or the basketball coach or saving our butts from the Wolf Lords.

Seems Dirk Daring, Secret Agent, was keeping secrets from his Noble Unicorn Colleague. Again. Still.

But not, if the Unicorn had anything to say about it, for long.

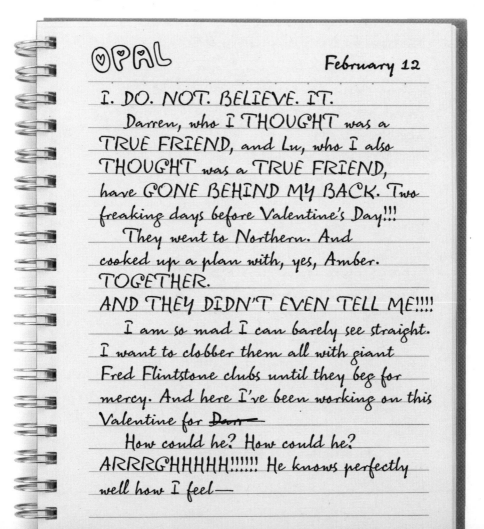

OPAL   February 12

I. DO. NOT. BELIEVE. IT.

Darren, who I THOUGHT was a TRUE FRIEND, and Lu, who I also THOUGHT was a TRUE FRIEND, have GONE BEHIND MY BACK. Two freaking days before Valentine's Day!!!

They went to Northern. And cooked up a plan with, yes, Amber. TOGETHER.

AND THEY DIDN'T EVEN TELL ME!!!!

I am so mad I can barely see straight. I want to clobber them all with giant Fred Flintstone clubs until they beg for mercy. And here I've been working on this Valentine for ~~Darr~~

How could he? How could he? ARRRGHHHHH!!!!!! He knows perfectly well how I feel—

But I guess he's just like everyone else, like his good buddy, that snake Travis. What does mom always say? Judge a person by the company he keeps?

So that's it for me. I am so done. Done done done with Dirk Daring and his idiot agent stuff. And with the Kitchen Cabinet and idiot Jason and his pompous b.s. and with stupid Lu and her stupid Scrabble and stupid Sudoku and stupid unicorn fixation like she's five years old.

It seems none of them remember that there's more to me than just this "pretty face" (gack!). I am a Vega, through and through. And a pissed Vega is a dangerous Vega. Those guys better watch their backs. Because I've got a little DIRK of my own (which I just found out is actually a kind of dagger). And it's absolutely perfect for inserting between the shoulder blades of my enemies.

Hamburger colossus evil empire hamster dear
wind willow rat ruby emerald opal amethyst
sapphire topaz wall curt will handspring burrito
breath binary stapler you android freight
knickers toot shenanigans be trial by fire wheat
hairball my knobby koala bear invisible rage
valentine tempest cord lope vandal triage your
cosmic loaf radish elevator skink friend cope
keep cop deep dope Darren[2]

---

2 E6 code—read every sixth word only.

Notes from Meeting with Agent Jewel.

LAF2LOL4HA886666ow De-encrypted. 2/13.

I can't say I've ever been a big fan of Valentine's Day. All that mushy, lovey-dovey stuff. Making all those stupid valentines for *everybody in the class.* As if this would change the fact that some kids are popular and some kids aren't. And getting a forced valentine is even worse than getting no valentine at all. Because it turns people's feelings into fakery and junk, good for nothing but the recycling bin.

That's how it always seemed to me, anyway.

Except for this year. Things were different now.

For the first time ever, there was someone I wanted to give a valentine to.

Yeah, life is weird.

I checked inside my notebook. Yes—it was still there, safely tucked between two blank pages. I had done some fancy cutting and pasting and Photoshopping to create a special card for you-know-who.

TOP SECRET VALENTINE

TO:
Agent
Allegra
Montefiore

FROM:
Agent
Dirk
Daring

MISSION INSTRUCTIONS:

- Meet at dead-drop location 15:45 hours as per secret communique to be delivered via text at 09:32 hours.
- Take delivery of 1 Confidential Valentine.
- Decode using E6 code.
- Reply using E3 Code.
- Retain until further notice.

Now I just had to summon up the guts to deliver it.

I got to school early. I positioned myself near Opal's locker, trying not to look too conspicuous. But my heart was thumping like a lopsided load in the washer. *Tha-rump, tha-rump, tha-rump.*

The hallway was crowded. I stood on my toes, searching.

Yes—there she was! Her gleaming white parka and sparkly purple hat appeared and disappeared, appeared and disappeared, among the crowd.

I was sorely tempted to just cut and run. But I didn't. I held my ground.

She arrived at my elbow. She didn't seem to notice me. She was too busy yanking off her backpack. Unwinding the bulky scarf that hid her face.

My heart upped its pace into spin-cycle double-time. *Thrumpa, thrumpa, thrumpa.*

Her scarf was finally unwound. Still Opal didn't notice me.

My face felt like it was glowing as hot and red as a—yes—valentine.

"Good morning, O.!" I said in my jauntiest, most confident voice. Or, rather, tried to say. It actually came out in a squeak.

And then Opal's scarf was off and her mittens were off and she slapped me across the face.

"Don't you ever, ever, *ever* talk to me again, Darren Dirkowitz! You backstabbing little...*argh*!!!"

She turned on her heel and ran off, leaving me clutching my stinging cheek, trying to swallow and wondering how everything could have gone so desperately, miserably wrong.

A Trap for a Unicorn.

With great care I don my hunting gear. Dark boots. Dark jacket. Dark hat.

With great care I add camouflage. Neutral face. Casual posture.

Only then do I enter the precinct of my quarry.

The elusive one.

My mission: To find this Unicorn. And trap it with its own bridle, its own shiny purple reins.

I will lead it, prancing, dancing, snorting, into the light. Or fall on my sword, defeated by an invincible, invisible equine enemy.

As. If.

I slide one foot, then the other, silently across the peaty turf. I turn my nose skyward. Sniff the air for any hint of horse.

Sniff.

Sniff.

Nothing but the dampish scent of winter. Of dead crabgrass and hot grease from the chip wagon parked at the curb.

Yet Dirk Daring, Secret Agent, has more than nose and eyes at his disposal. He has the keenest of insight. The deepest understanding of psychology.

And horse sense. In spades. Neigh.

There—I see the Unicorn, in shining ivory glory.

My prey.

"Hey," I say.

The elusive creature startles.

"Oh. Hi."

"I know your secret," I say.

"Which one?"

"You told Opal. About going to see Amber."

"Er, yeah. Sorry 'bout that. Accident."

"Accident?" I snort. "Yeah right."

"It was! It just slipped out."

Her eyes slide to mine. A familiar frisson runs up my spine.

We have played this game before, this conspirator and I. She is not one to be trifled with.

"No. You told her on purpose," I said.

"Don't be an idiot. Why would I do that?"

"Don't know. But you did."

Her jaw lifts. Thrusts forward in a defensive parry.

"So I spilled the beans. What about it?" She draws a circle in the dirt with the toe of her shiny pink boot.

"Just wondering why."

Her eyes narrow, and she strikes.

"Why not? I mean, you guys are supposed to be my friends. But I know what you both think—what a joke Lu is, with her Scrabble and Sudoku and loud laugh. Yes, I know you think I have an awful laugh, Darren. Yours isn't exactly music either, you know."

I don't let her petty distraction distract me. I have a greater purpose. For Dirk Daring, Secret Agent, sees Opportunity where others only see twinkling unicorn turds.

She strikes again, wielding her sharp words like flashing swords.

"And if that's not bad enough, there you are, going all sappy over Opal. It's kinda disgusting, Darren, if you really want to know. Besides, I thought it would be fun. To mess with some heads."

Your head, she means.

But the head of Dirk Daring, Secret Agent, cannot be messed with.

When she realizes her attack misses its mark, Fury's face crumples.

"Wait—you're not going to…? No—you wouldn't."

"Wouldn't what?" I say with utmost patience. I am still, after all, stalking my quarry.

"Out me. Tell Opal. Jason. Everybody."

I point to my chest. Raise my eyebrows.

She sighs a great big unicorn sigh.

"No, I guess you wouldn't. Not after—because you know what it feels like…you wouldn't do that to someone else…"

"My lips are sealed, Lu. For now. But you owe me. And Opal. Don't forget it."

I leave the Unicorn with that unpleasant debt to ponder. And go to collect on yet another debt. One still outstanding with Dirk Daring, Secret Agent.

I caught up to Travis in front of Bo Diddley Burger and Shake Drive-In.

"Yo," I called out.

He froze. Gave me a wary half grin.

"Hey," he said. "Sorry if I seem a little…tense. I keep expecting to get jumped by God-knows-who every time I leave my house. Heck, every time I go into my house."

I nodded. Looked away.

Travis took a step toward me.

"Darren? I heard about that Opal thing. Sorry, man."

I felt my throat tighten up again. It had been doing that all day.

"I warned you she was, you know, *woo-woo*." He twirled his finger near his ear.

I took a step back.

"I'm not here to talk about Opal," I said. "Seems you owe me—and Jason—an explanation."

His eyes fell.

He mumbled, "I don't know what you mean."

"Yeah, you do. You stole those math tests—the ones you sold to Jason—from his room. And then you gave them to Bonaparte. Which he then proceeded to use as leverage. To bully Jason. Until we stopped him, that is."

Travis's eyes darted left, right. "Do we have to have this conversation here? Like, in the middle of the sidewalk?"

I didn't move a muscle. Didn't blink an eye.

I confess, I relished his discomfiture.

Travis sighed. "Okay, so I guess we do." He made a gooselike motion with his neck. "Yeah. I did steal the test. Grabbed the test papers right out of his room. The very same day I discovered that can of spray paint. In your room."

Now it was my turn to feel discomfited.

Last fall, I had used that can of paint to forge Travis's signature drawing, Surfer Dude, on the inside of a bathroom stall. My little act of betrayal had gotten him a month's detention.

"I was so bleepin' mad you did that!" Travis said. "I wanted to beat the living daylights out of you! I wanted to turn you into Dirk pulp! Into Daring pudding! Into Deadbeat, Dead Dog, Dead Darren Soup!"

I felt my ears go red.

He gave me that lopsided grin again.

"Lucky for you I'm not a punch-you-out kind of guy, eh?"

That stopped me short. *Was* it lucky for me?

Who could say?

Maybe things would have turned out better if he *had* beaten me to a pulp back then.

Because this—*this*—this never-ending stomach twist of not trusting Travis but still wishing we were friends—was pretty much my definition of hell.

And now that Opal hated me and Lu had proven herself, once again, to be untrustworthy, let's just say I missed Travis's friendship more than ever. Jason was no substitute.

"I was so mad, and I so wanted revenge," Travis went on. "But I didn't know how to get back at you. I did know how to get back at Waldo though. I knew his weak spot. Hadn't I sold him those very tests?

"Besides, Bonaparte had been crawling up my butt. Telling me how he was gonna have me expelled for vandalism. I needed something to get him off my back.

"Giving him that test? Okay, I'm not proud of it. But that was back then. You know, before. I wouldn't do it now. You gotta believe me."

He reached out, touched my sleeve.

"Darren? You gotta believe me."

I met his eyes. Swirling, dark pools of misery.

Probably mine didn't look much different.

In that moment, I realized I did.

Believe him, that is.

Travis *had* changed. Or maybe he had just grown up since October.

This new-and-improved Travis really didn't mean to hurt people. In fact, he was doing everything he could to make things right again.

Even so…

He *had* stolen the test. And the Student Council money.

He was trouble.

You might as well pin a giant blinking warning on the guy: *Danger! Handle at your own risk.*

So the question remained.

Could I trust this rash, reckless, pathetic excuse for a friend, even if he meant well?

On the other hand...

Who else could I trust?

Not Lu.

Not Jason.

Not Opal.

I wasn't even really sure I could trust myself.

Truth was, we were all thieves and liars. Hadn't we all been taking—stealing—money that didn't belong to us, week after week after week, with our phony fundraisers?

Travis wasn't any different from the rest of us. Fear had turned us all into fraud artists.

My gut twisted one notch tighter.

I said, "We can't keep this up, you know. Turning ourselves inside out like this. For them. Before long we'll *be* them."

Travis let out a huge sigh.

"Too true. And here's another thing. I think Conner's

getting deeper in every day. So deep he won't be able to get out. And he *is* my brother. Even though he's a creep, like it or not, he's family.

"I'm scared, D. For me. For him. For all of us."

His words hit me hard.

What kind of person would I be if I turned away from him now?

Not someone I wanted to be.

I felt the lump that had been sitting like a black toad on my heart since autumn begin to shrivel.

A new lump grew, this time in my throat.

"This sucks," I said, my voice barely more than a whisper.

"You'll never know just how sorry I am." Travis turned his face away. Swiped at his cheek with the back of his hand.

I knew I needed to give him space. To save whatever face he had left.

"I've got an idea," I lied. "Meet me inside Bo Diddley in five minutes." I pivoted on my heel and rushed into the diner. Wiped away some random raindrops that had somehow found their way to my own cheeks.

The diner's impersonal clamor wrapped around me like a warm blanket. I slid into Travis's and my favorite booth. I closed my eyes and let my heart rate return to something approaching normal. I felt...

I don't know what I felt.

Scared. Sad. Excited. Vindicated. Lonely. Not lonely. Dumb.

Maybe that's what people mean when they say they feel *alive.*

I ordered two chocolate milkshakes. One for me and one for Travis. His double chocolate, just the way he liked it.

Still no sign of him. I fished a pen from my knapsack and grabbed a fistful of napkins from the shiny metal dispenser. I had some thinking to do, and doodling always helped me think.

I unfolded one napkin. Laid it flat on the Formica tabletop. Carefully, so as not to tear the paper, I drew a rough chart on it.

An idea fluttered into my brain.

I sucked on my straw and stared out the window, letting the idea flutter close enough to grasp.

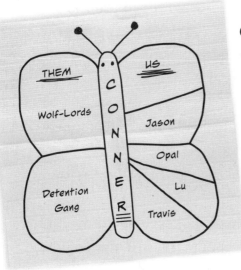

I underlined the name *Conner* on my napkin. Once. Twice. Three times.

Travis slipped into the booth opposite me. His face was drawn, but his eyes were dry.

He curled his hand around the tall metal cup. "Thanks, D. I owe you one. More than one."

Yeah, he did. But I decided to keep that thought to myself.

Last fall I'd discovered that speaking up was good. Necessary, even. But now, I realized, speaking your mind also had a downside. Once spoken, words couldn't be unspoken. And you couldn't forgive if you never gave yourself a chance to forget.

Sometimes the right thing to do was leave some things unsaid.

I told Travis, "Forget it. We have more important things to discuss." His lip quivered. His eyes went *blinkety-blink, blinkety-blink.*

"Yeah. Well. Thanks." He took a long, deep, noisy slurp on his straw.

My eyes drifted back to the napkin with my doodles on it. The plan, coming together.

Travis jerked his chin toward the sketch.

"So? Does that have something to do with your idea?"

"Yeah…I think so." I tapped the chart with the tip of my pencil. "You know how we conned the Detention Gang? Made them fall into our trap with just the right bait?"

Travis laughed. "Yeah—Opal waving around her new purse full of 'money.' They fell for it hook, line and sinker."

"Well, I'm thinking the only way out of this mess is to do the same thing again. But on a bigger scale. A total scorched-earth, leave-no-man-standing con game. Or shall we say a 'Conner Game.'"

Travis laughed. The real, old-fashioned, Travis laugh. I hadn't heard it in months.

"You mean con Conner?"

"And the rest of 'em too. We can't outmuscle 'em. But we can outthink them."

Travis leaned back in his seat. He wiped a dribble of chocolate from his chin. He rubbed his hands together gleefully.

"Oh, baby! Does that ever sound like a mission for D—"

"Nuh-uh. I can't do this alone, Travis. It's too complicated."

I fiddled with the napkin, folding it and unfolding it absently while I thought everything through.

"I need a partner. Someone clever and canny and a little bit—no, a lot bit—twisted. Someone who will go too far and cross the line. A really practiced liar who will take some really, really stupid chances for the team."

Travis's upper lip twitched. "You mean it? Because if you do, I may know someone who fits the bill, Dirk."

"I just might too, T-Bone. I just might too."

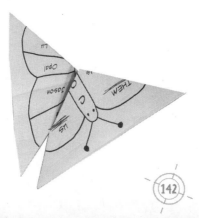

February 14

Little Miss Trust

It starts with the smallest betrayal
A jab
"This won't hurt a bit!"
A jest
"I was just kidding,
God you are so sensitive!"

Which expands into a
Pandemic of
Punishment

"Don't be such a baby"
"You make me sick."

And spreads ♡OPAL
To everyone
You know.

"It's not what you think!"
"I didn't mean anything by it!"

An ebola of hurt.

Dirk Daring's Strategic Alliances Chart
Revised

TOP SECRET

ICON (name)	FIRM ALLY	Neutral/Unstable ALLIANCE	SWORN ENEMY
JEWEL		Waldo, T-Bone	Double Trouble, Fury, Dirk, BEAST
FURY	Dirk, Waldo	Double Trouble, Jewel, T-Bone	BEAST
WALDO		Dirk, Fury, Jewel, Double Trouble, T-Bone	BEAST
T-BONE	Dirk	Double Trouble	BEAST
Bonaparte		Fancy Boots, Outrage, Waldo, Exasperation	Dirk, T-Bone
Exasperation			Fancy Boots, Outrage, Waldo, Dirk, T-Bone, Fury, Jewel, Bonaparte
Fancy Boots			Outrage
Outrage	Double Trouble	Jewel	Fancy Boots
Double Trouble	T-bone		BEAST, Jewel
Dirk Daring	CLASSIFIED	CLASSIFIED	CLASSIFIED

COACH ANTHONY GREGORI: (basketball coach, Northern Senior Public School) <singing along with radio> Run to the hills, run for your li-ii-ife...

<knocking sound>

COACH: Ahem. Come in! Ah! Zeb! Archie! Nice to see you! Here, sit. (sound of rustling papers, clearing of chairs?) Sit.

MALE VOICE 1 (Zeb? Archie?): We just thought we'd pop by. We were in the neighborhood. And you know how grateful we are that you run such a great sports program here at Northern.

COACH: Why, thank you! It's been a real pleasure. Let me tell you, a real pleasure.

MALE VOICE 1: Wyatt just loves basketball. Speaks very highly of you too.

MALE VOICE 2 (Zeb? Archie?): So does Benji.

COACH: And they are great kids, lemme tell you. I really love having them on the team. The Bobcats would be in the cellar without them.

MALE VOICE 1: Wyatt's having a great year.

COACH: Not bad. Not bad at all. He still needs work on his outside shooting. But all in all, he's progressing nicely. Benji too, Zeb. A good team player, your son.

MALE VOICE 2 (Zeb): Glad to hear it. Glad to hear it.

ARCHIE: Which is why, ahem, we wanted to pop in and say hi.

\<scratching sound\>

COACH: Oh?

ARCHIE: You see there, heh-heh, Wyatt complains that he doesn't get enough court time.

COACH: Well, you know court ti—

ARCHIE: And he thinks you maybe don't put kids out based on who deserves it.

COACH: I have to give everybody on the team a chance out there, Arch. You know that.

ZEB: 'Course you do, Coach. But even so. We've heard some, ahem, rumors.

COACH: Rumors?

ZEB: That you are open to, shall we say, encouragement?

<paper rustling, rubber band snapping>

ARCH: To help you decide who gets out there. To rack up the minutes. Which they need if they have any, you know...

ZEB: Scholarship hopes.

COACH: Er—

ARCH: And we understand too that scouts are coming through here in the next few weeks?

ZEB: I heard Villanova. Purdue. Duke.

COACH: Well, yes...there may in fact be a few scouts stopping in. From powerhouse colleges like those.

ARCH: And wouldn't that be great, just great, if Wyatt was on the court when the Duke scout was watching?

<sound of riffling paper>

ZEB: I'd say that would be wonderful. A whole fistful of wonderful.

<more riffling, sound of something sliding across wood>

ARCH: And another whole fistful if Benji were out there too. You know how well our boys play together. They been bouncing those b-balls off the house together since they were knee high to a grasshopper.

COACH: Well, I certainly take your point, fellas. Watching your boys play together is a thing to behold. Those scouts certainly should get to see them in action.

ARCH: It's all about court time. Which, of course, you will determine the best way you see fit.

ZEB: What's best for the team.

COACH: Always. What's best for the team. Thanks so much for dropping by, guys. I so enjoy receiving your, ah, input.

<sound of slapping, laughter>

<indecipherable>

COACH: Ciao!

<door opening, door closing>

<riffling sound>

<drawer opening, drawer closing>

COACH: <humming, tune of "Run for the Hills">

Notes from Meeting with T-Bone and Fury.
MA34!2G765 De-encrypted. 2/16.

Travis, Lu and I were doing homework together. Yeah, I know. Not exactly a recipe for peace and harmony, but we all wanted to keep one eye on—or ear on—the audio recorder.

With the skill and deviance of a future hacker god, Travis had set up the device Amber had concealed in the coach's office so that it continuously uploaded to the cloud. We could access said cloud from my desktop computer and review the audio at the end of the day. Or we could listen to it in real time. Which is why we were all doing math, elbow to elbow, sprawled out on my bedroom rug.

Well, all except Lu, who had finished her problem set and was now drawing, yes, unicorns.

I was halfway through my 33 assigned two-digit-decimals problems when the sound of a hunting horn—*Too doo! Too doo!!*—blasted from my desktop.

"What the heck?" Lucinda said.

"That's the alert! For the audio recorder! That means it's picking something up right now!" I reached across to the nearest speaker and turned the volume up.

"…know how grateful we are that you run such a great sports program here at Northern…"

Lu squealed, "It's working!"

Travis put his finger to his lips. "Shhh!"

We listened intently.

"…complains that he doesn't get enough court time…open to, shall we say, encouragement?…another whole fistful…"

Lu's eyes went as round as big brown Morning Glory muffins. "Oh. My. God," she mouthed.

"You know how well our boys play together…Thanks so much for dropping by, guys. I so enjoy receiving your, ah, input."

When the recording went quiet, I twisted the volume knob back to low.

"That was money I heard, right? Being riffled like this?" Lucinda gestured with her hands.

"Seems like it," I said.

Travis shook his head. "So there we have it again. The love of money equals root of all evil. Put that down on your math worksheet."

"So now what?" Lu asked. "I mean, I think it's really awesome and everything that we caught this guy red-handed being a crook"—Lucinda shot a sideways look at Travis—"but I'm not sure how we can use this. Wasn't the idea that we'd catch the *Wolf Lords* doing the bribing or blackmailing or whatever?"

I nodded. "Yeah, that's the plan. So now we sit tight and hope we catch—"

Travis's cell phone *bing*ed. He glanced at it and said, "Gotta take this."

He left the room. From out in the hall, I heard him say, "Hey."

Then nothing but the rise and fall of his voice.

Lu's lips drew together. She jabbed her thumb toward the door.

"And what do you think that's about, huh? He can't talk on the phone in front of us? He's playing us again, Darren! I just know it! Up to no good!"

My gut did a strange two-step.

Was Lu right? Was he talking with Conner? Reporting back to him? Betraying us?

I could hear Travis whispering in the hall. The rhythm of his words was insistent, urgent.

No, I told myself. *Don't let Lu stir up your doubts.*

I would trust him. I *had to* trust him.

He was sliding the phone into his pocket when he came back. His face had gone a strange color—a cross between squashed strawberry and blood.

He said, "About that audio? And what we should do next? Seems we don't have quite as many options as we thought."

Lu's face squinched. "Hunh? Why?"

"That was Amber."

No wonder he'd wanted privacy, knowing how he felt about her. Hadn't I felt the same way about—

I forced the image of Opal—her hand slinging toward my cheek—out of my mind.

I couldn't, wouldn't, think about Opal now. Ever.

Travis said, "She was carrying pylons from jv practice back to the storage room when she saw these two guys go into Coach Gregori's office. She smelled some serious rat stink. Thought she'd hang around a min. Hear what went down with her own two ears."

"You mean Amber was there? Right now? Like, while we were listening too?" Lu gave a little shiver. "That's, like, too weird."

"And?" I asked.

"And so as soon as they all left, she said she went into the office and snagged the bug."

"What? Why?" Lu said. "No one told her to do that!"

Travis gave a dry laugh. "Come on, Lu. You should know—nobody tells Amber what to do. Amber does what Amber wants to do."

"What does Amber plan to do with the bug then?"

"She says she's gonna make sure it gets to the principal first thing tomorrow."

"Nooooo! That won't help us stop the Wolf Lords!" Lu cried.

"No, it won't. Which is what I was trying to tell her. But she says she cares most about basketball and Northern and wants that coach gone."

My heart did a strange double bump. The puzzle pieces falling into place. That sick look on Travis's face.

I said, "So she's hanging you out to dry, Travis."

"I wouldn't go that far," he said, running one hand casually through his hair. But his face was the color of pancake batter.

Fine. I'd let him keep his one shred of hope. I knew how bad it felt when that last shred was cut.

I said, "Let's look at the bright side. The mission isn't a total bust. When this gets out, the school merger will be deader than a duck in orange sauce. They can't bring in a whole new whack of students while they clean house."

"Okay. There's that," Travis said. "But still. I thought we were almost out from under the Wolf-Lord shadow."

Lu's shoulders slumped. "Instead we're back to square one. On our most importantest mission."

Travis and I exchanged a look.

"Not exactly," I said.

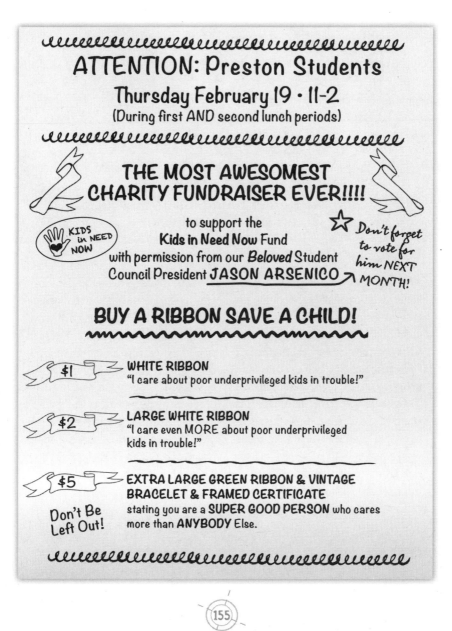

ATTENTION: Preston Students
Thursday February 19 · 11-2
(During first AND second lunch periods)

THE MOST AWESOMEST CHARITY FUNDRAISER EVER!!!!

KIDS in NEED NOW

to support the
Kids in Need Now Fund
with permission from our *Beloved* Student
Council President **JASON ARSENICO**

☆ Don't forget to vote for him NEXT MONTH!

BUY A RIBBON SAVE A CHILD!

$1 — **WHITE RIBBON**
"I care about poor underprivileged kids in trouble!"

$2 — **LARGE WHITE RIBBON**
"I care even MORE about poor underprivileged kids in trouble!"

$5 — **EXTRA LARGE GREEN RIBBON & VINTAGE BRACELET & FRAMED CERTIFICATE**
stating you are a **SUPER GOOD PERSON** who cares more than **ANYBODY** Else.

Don't Be Left Out!

PRESTON PRESTIGE

BASKETBALL COACH BOUNCED!!!

Caught Red-Handed Taking Bribes

BY LUCINDA LEE, STAFF REPORTER

ANTHONY GREGORI, THE HEAD basketball coach at Northern Senior Public School, was suspended indefinitely yesterday after evidence surfaced that he was taking bribes from parents. The bribes were paid to him to ensure that certain students would be given more than their fair share of court time during Bobcat basketball games over the next few weeks, when college scouts will be evaluating players in order to determine who will be offered scholarships worth upwards of $100,000.

The evidence came in the form of a digital recording device, which appeared on the desk of Northern's principal, Mrs. Alvina Ferrer, yesterday morning during second period. A typed note saying, "This is what's going on in your sports program" was taped to the "bug." Neither of the secretaries were in the office at the time, having both "stepped away from their desks" to deal with school business elsewhere. Mrs. Ferrer had just given a short speech to the grade 11 French class on senior study opportunities in Aix-en-Provence and returned to her desk to find the device front and center.

Mrs. Ferrer reportedly listened to the audio recording and immediately recognized the voices of Coach Gregori and two parents of players on the team. She would not release the names of those parents, who really should be ashamed of themselves.

According to Ferrer's official statement, "Coach Gregori will be removed from his duties while we conduct a formal investigation of this matter. No students will be disciplined at this time, and Northern's Bobcats basketball program will continue without interruption under the direction of Assistant Coach Bob Gamble."

Students at Northern were both shocked and disgusted by the news. "No wonder our team sucked," said junior Ridley Wechsler. "He played who paid."

"He always looked at me funny," said one member of the female JV squad, who wouldn't give her name. "I never did trust him. Now I know he was scum."

Sophomore Sophia Wozniak said, "What I wanna know is, who put the bug in his office? They're, like, a hero."

Her friend Gina Schmidt, also a sophomore, agreed. "Yeah, they should get a medal or something."

When the question of who planted the bug was put to members of the boys' varsity basketball team, no one would answer this reporter's questions. The most I could get out of them came from Wyatt Zappa, team captain: "No comment. Now go away, twerp."

Northern's next basketball game will be February 18 (that's tomorrow, people!) at 6 PM. They will be playing the Trevalyan Tigers. Anyone who likes excitement and drama, both on and off the court, and who hates people who call other people twerps should attend! Go, Tigers!

♡OPAL

Still

Still (noun):
A device for separation.

Still (adjective):
Unmoving, unmoved.

To Still (verb):
To make silent

And Still (adverb):
You have not come back.

Notes from Unplanned Meeting with Opal.
90453DFK-G1 De-encrypted. 2/19.

I sat at the sale table in the main hall, a brightly false smile on my face. Kids groaned as they passed. I didn't blame them a bit.

It was one thing to fork over funds for a delicious brownie. And another to do it just to wear a stupid ribbon on your shirt.

But Lu and Opal had insisted—when they were still speaking to each other—that we could make the ribbons a new thing. A status symbol. And once it became the "must-have" fashion statement, kids would give their right eye to get one.

The only eye anybody was giving me, though, was the dead eye.

Even worse, there I was, sitting thigh to thigh with Opal. Not talking to her. Not looking at her. Pretending I didn't notice her seething beside me.

I'd tried time and time again to break through her snow cone of silence. To tell her she was wrong, that I hadn't betrayed her. But she'd given me no way in.

And then I thought, Why bother? A real friend wouldn't have cut me dead the way she had. Not without giving me a chance to explain. And then—she'd hit me! That was too far. Way too far.

So there we sat, perfectly paired pillars of hurt and resentment.

Fun, fun, fun.

Yet we *had* to do this. The flimsy ribbons we were flogging were all that stood between us and certain pulverization.

Feeling like a giant jerk, I shouted, "Come on, folks, step right up, don't be shy! Show how much you care! All sales to a totally great cause!"

A couple of guys stopped their horsing around. They exchanged a cryptic look and sidled up to Opal.

"How much for a ribbon?" one asked.

"A dollar for the small ones, $2 for the bigger white ones, and $5 for the green. You get a bracelet and a certificate of awesome person-ness with those," Opal said. Without much enthusiasm.

He held one of the ribbons up to his shirt pocket. Said in falsetto, "Does it go with my blouse?"

The other guy sniggered. "It enhances your eyes. Really. I mean that from deep in my heart. My left ventricle."

"Come on, guys, don't be goofs. These ribbons are important," Opal said. There were deep shadows under her eyes. She looked like she hadn't slept in a week.

She looked like she was *this close* to snapping.

"Yeah. Right. Like buying one of these from you guys is really gonna make a difference," he said, snorting.

He tossed the ribbon back on the table, then swaggered away, laughing and exchanging stupid cracks with his pal.

At our expense.

That was the last straw.

I shoved myself back from the table. "Those guys are right," I said, getting to my feet. "I'm tired of fleecing people. See you later."

I tried to edge around the table, but Opal grabbed my wrist. "Oh no you don't. Quit trying to sneak your way out of things, *Dirk*."

I spluttered. "Sneak out of things? What are you talking about?"

"You're in as long as you can play Mr. Secret Spy Dude, sneaking around, making yourself feel all important. But when the going gets tough"—she waved her hand at the table of unsold ribbons—"off you go, leaving your so-called friends to do the dirty work."

I could feel my cheeks burning. I was mad, all right, but also hurt.

Which meant I didn't stop to think about my next words. I just reacted. Badly.

"Is that so, Miss Perfecty-Perfect?" I yelled. "You don't exactly pull *your* weight either. You just sit around and roll your eyes and find fault. Pick, pick, pick. And what have you done? You haven't even baked anything since the first week. Who do you think made those brownies? Elves?"

I yanked my arm from her grip. Her fingernails left pale white lines on my skin. "Jason is right—you really are that *B* word."

Opal's mouth gaped. Glassy droplets beaded on her lower eyelid.

"Look who's calling who names now, Mr. Coward! Mr. Stalker! Mr. Liar!" Her whole body shook, her face as red as a broken heart.

A crowd gathered around us. Nothing better than a good fight, was there?

"Oh yeah?" I shouted at Opal. "Well, you're not exactly the Queen of Honest!" I was breathing so hard, the words came out in harsh staccato blats.

Travis shot me a look that said, *Sorry, dude, but business is business.*

He stepped between us and the mob and called out, "Step right up, folks! Buy a ribbon, get the best spot to witness the excitement! Opal and Darren in a lovers' quarrel! At each other's throats! Five ribbons, five bucks, gets you primo location in the front row!"

Opal's eyes flicked from me to Travis and back again. Utter loathing transformed her features, twisting them into a quivering knot. Even her hair shimmied and shook.

"Now look what you've done!" she screamed.

"Fight!" someone yelled out. "Fight! Go on, give it to him, Opal!"

"Me?" I screamed at her. "It was you! You started it!"

"No, you did! With your lying, cheating—"

Someone else took up the chant. "Fight, fight, fight!"

Kids handed Travis money. Fistfuls of coins.

Opal stamped her foot. "Stop it! Stop it right now, all of you!" Tears swelled in her eyes and broke loose. They cascaded down her cheeks in two perfect, parallel lines. Her face twisted yet again, this time into a mask of anguish.

I didn't know what to do. I was so mad, so crazy upset with her, with myself, with everything and everybody. But I did know we couldn't keep standing there like that while the whole school laughed at us and egged us on.

I grabbed Opal's hand. I shouldered my way past Travis, dragging Opal with me.

"Let go of me!" Opal railed.

"Just shut up. We're getting out of here. Pronto." I frog-marched her down the hall, away from the mob.

"Don't go now! We're finally getting rid of these ribbons!" Travis shouted after us.

I dragged Opal past the cafeteria. Shouts of "You got this, Darren!" and "Aw, come on, just when things were getting good!" echoed around us.

LET SLEEPING DOGS LIE

We quick-stepped as fast as we could without letting ourselves break into a run. If we ran…well, it would be game over.

The turnoff to the south corridor was just ahead. If we could only get there before we were surrounded again…

Quick step, quick step, quick step. We swung around the corner. There, on our left, was the art-supply cupboard. I twisted the knob. Miracle of miracles—it was unlocked!

"Opal! In here!"

We slipped inside. I shut the door behind us with a quiet click.

Inside, it was pitch-black. The air was warm, close, like a held breath. In that tiny space, we had no choice but to press up against each other.

I could feel Opal's narrow shoulders shaking.

"It's okay, it's okay," I said, all my anger suddenly spent. My arms, as if by their own design, went around her shoulders.

We heard feet thundering down the corridor. Then voices:

"Where'd they go?"

"Crap. Show's over."

"Guess we'll have to do our science lab report. No fair."

I heard a few groans, and then the footsteps and squealing and giddy laughter faded away.

In our dark silence, I could literally feel Opal trying to get a hold of herself. It wasn't working. She was still trembling.

"I'm not going back out there. Ever," she choked out.

I nodded, even though she couldn't see me. "Me neither. Not till the bell rings. At least." I could smell her shampoo. Something peachy.

"Maybe not even then," she sniffled. "God, that was so humiliating." I felt her collapse in on herself—all the fight had gone out of her. She was just Opal again. Sad, hurt Opal.

My Jewel.

I lifted one hand and felt the wall beside the door until I found the light switch. I snapped it on.

The light shone down like a prison spotlight. It caught us out with our arms wrapped around each other. Her cheek against my temple.

Awkward.

I untangled my arms. Levered my body away from hers.

There. A nice safe distance between us. *Whew.*

Still, my whole body felt like I'd been zapped by a cattle prod. Every single hair was standing on end.

I couldn't look at Opal. Instead, I checked out our hidey-hole. It was lined wall to wall with racking. Plastic tubs full of odds and ends, scraps and tools filled the shelves.

A green plastic tub labeled *Felt squares, pipe cleaners, etc.* sat like a fat toad on the bottom shelf. I yanked it free and patted it with my open hand.

"Here. Sit."

She sat.

I pulled out a second tub, this one labeled *Patterned scrap paper/Holiday themes.* I sank down onto it, forcing my elbows tight to my sides, pressing my knees together. Acutely aware of Opal, sitting just inches away.

"Now isn't this funner than a barrel of monkeys," I said. Lightly, like it was a joke. But my heart was thumping like a herd of rhinos. The tension? You could cut it with a you-know-what.

Opal took a deep, deep breath. Let it out with a *whhhft.*

"I'm sorry, D. I shouldn't have said those things to you. Especially not in front of"—she waved her arm toward "out there"—"the hyenas."

"Yeah. Well. You were upset." *Not quite forgiveness.*

She shot me a sideways look. "Yeah. I was. *Am.*"

I saw the tears welling in her eyes again. Her lower lip, her chin, trembled. "How could you, Darren? Go see Amber, without even telling me? You know how I-I..."

She cupped one hand over her eyes.

I just sat there, feeling like a tool. Wanting to comfort her. Not knowing how.

"I did know. Do know," I finally said. "But it's not what you think..."

"And Lu! Of all people! You took that little weaselly sneak with you! *Arrgh*! How could you!"

I could see she was winding herself up again and would really launch into me in just 3...2...1...

"*Argh!!!* How could I have been such an idiot! To even think of trusting y—"

"Opal! Stop! Just shut up and listen for a second, okay? I'm trying to tell you something! But it isn't easy."

She gave me another sideways look. "Go on."

"I couldn't take you! Because I...well, I needed to talk to Amber alone. Without you."

I heard the catch in her throat. "I knew it. You and Amber and Travis...all ganging up on me..."

"Nobody's ganging up on you, Opal. I know I'm saying this all wrong. But gimme a chance, okay? Please just listen!"

Opal wiped her face with the back of one fist.

"Okay," she said miserably.

"I didn't tell you I was going to see Amber because I knew you'd kill me if you knew what I was planning to do."

"Er, yah..."

"But I didn't see any other way. I know she doesn't talk to you directly anymore. And that sucks. Totally sucks."

"Tell me about it," she whispered.

"So I thought maybe if I talked to her? Told her how you felt? She might, you know, smarten up."

Opal lifted her face and gaped at me. Her mouth was a perfect round O. Her cheeks were tear stained. Blotchy.

She still looked amazing.

I struggled to get the words out. "I thought I could make things better. For you. If I could give you Amber as, you know, a Valentine's present."

Her eyebrows lifted. So high they practically hit her perfect hairline.

I dropped my eyes. "But I'm an idiot. A jerk, just like you said. And a failure. I blew it. I'm sorry," I said into my lap.

"You mean you went there for me? To try to get her to make up? With me?"

"Yeah." I shifted my weight on the tub. "Also to give her the listening device. But Travis could have done that easy peasy. But I wouldn't let him. So yeah. For that."

"What did she say?"

I shrugged my shoulders. "Not much, really."

Opal's shoulders slumped.

"I'd kinda hoped she'd think about what I said, at least, and that she'd decide to kiss and make up with you, so to speak. You know. For Valentine's." I shook my head. "The way you two are not talking is just…ridick."

"She didn't," Opal said.

"I kinda figured that. By your, um, reaction." My hand rose to my cheek. The one Opal had slapped.

We sat side by side in silence. Not moving. Hardly even breathing.

I studied the rack of posterboard, all the colors sorted so neatly, like a rainbow. If only real life were as easy to sort out.

"I'm so sorry, Darren. I should have never done that. Slapped you, I mean. It was just. Well. I didn't know."

"I know you didn't. I tried to tell you! But you wouldn't even give me a chance! And then, well, you hit me. And that made me mad. Really mad. That's why I called you that name. I didn't mean it. Not really."

"I guess I don't blame you." She put her hand on top of mine. "What I did was wrong."

Another long, awkward silence.

"And you were right, Darren. Out there. When you called me that name. I have been kind of a…*that* lately."

"No, you haven't," I lied, because I suddenly didn't care anymore. About who did what, who said what.

She was holding my hand.

I could barely breathe.

"It's just that I've been so down. About Amber. About this whole Wolf-Lord thing. I can hardly think straight. Sometimes I feel like I'm about to drown."

"You don't have to explain. I get it. Really."

She raised her eyes to mine. Gave me a soul-searching look. A soul-*searing* look.

Something cracked open inside me.

"You do, don't you, Darren? I mean, you always seem to know, to understand, exactly what I'm thinking. And I feel like I know exactly what you're thinking too."

I think my heart stopped beating when she said that.

A glimmer of a smile lifted the corners of her lips. "It's strange, isn't it?"

"Yeah," I said. I tried to swallow, but my throat was dry as toast.

"And it was always like that between us, wasn't it? Right from the very beginning. When we first became friends. It's like we have this special bond between us that lets us see inside each other to the real person underneath, and that makes words unnecessary."

I think I made a weird sort of choking sound then. Either Opal didn't notice, or she thought it was my caveman way of agreeing.

"Most people act like, *Oh, a pretty girl like you, you must not have any brains in that empty dolly head of yours!* And everything is fine as long as you don't make 'trouble' by having the nerve to want more. But I do, Darren! I want more. I deserve more!"

I could see by the way her jaw jutted out, the way her shoulders hunched, that she'd had this conversation with herself before.

"But you never did that, D. Act like I was some bubblehead Disney-princess wannabe. Not once. You always act like I have something worth saying."

"Well, you do," I managed to stutter.

"You see what I mean?" She laughed again, then nudged me gently with her shoulder. "You see me. The real me, underneath. Don't you?"

Her face was inches from mine, and her breath smelled sweetly of grape bubblegum. I think maybe I passed out for a second, because I kind of disappeared while everything seemed to just—stop. But then I heard her fingers scrabbling for the light switch, and the room went black.

And the next bit? Well, that's not something I'm ever going to commit to paper.

No, sir.

A smart guy knows when to keep his mouth shut.

WALDO: So you asked to see me, Principal Lipschitz?

BONAPARTE: Yes. Come in, son. Sit. Valerie! Will you join us, please?

‹shuffling, squeaking›

BONAPARTE: So. ‹sound of pencil tapping on desk›

We have some news for you. Very good news.

WALDO: Oh?

BONAPARTE: I got a message this morning from the board office. The members of the board were very impressed, they say, with the "school spirit" shown by Preston students at the school merger meeting.

WALDO: Oh!

BONAPARTE: And with, ahem, my "exemplary" leadership.

‹smothered noises—snort? Guffaw? Indecipherable.›

WALDO: Ohhhhhh.....

EXASPERATION: Cut to the chase already, Nate. The merger is <expletive: deleted> kaput.

WALDO: Oh?

BONAPARTE: Completely.

EXASPERATION: The scandal over at Northern scotched it for good. So here we all are. Stuck with each other.

<shuffling sound, squashing sound, squeaking sounds>

BONAPARTE: <giggling> Valerie!

WALDO: Ms. Wycoff! Should you, er, be doing that here? In front of me?

EXASPERATION: Relax, kid. He's got something else to tell you.

WALDO: Oh?

BONAPARTE: You know how Va—er, Ms. Wycoff has been out this last few weeks? With the shingles? Well, we realized during this time of separation exactly how much we depend on each other. I asked her to marry me. She said—

EXASPERATION: Yes. I said yes. So we're getting hitched and moving to the sunny south. I <expletive: deleted> hate winter.

WALDO: Oh!

BONAPARTE: Don't worry, son. We're not moving on until next year. We'll both be here for your grade 8 grad.

WALDO: Oh.

"So let's give ourselves a round of applause," Jason said. "The school merger is dead. Finito. Heard it straight from the horse's mouth."

"Woo and hoo!" Opal said, her fist in the air. "Score one for the Kitchen Cabinet."

"That's one less thing to worry about," Lu said. She bit her lip. "Not that we're out of the woods. We still have the Wolf Lords to deal with."

Travis turned to Jason. "We may have a way out of that."

Jason leaned in. "Oh?"

"Uh-huh. Darren and I have come up with a plan. To beat the Wolf Lords. At their own game."

Travis beckoned us with his finger, urging everyone to lean in even closer. "It's totally, completely, freaking awesome. Right, D.?"

"Indeed," I said. "Stellar."

"So. Can we trust you all to keep quiet about this?"

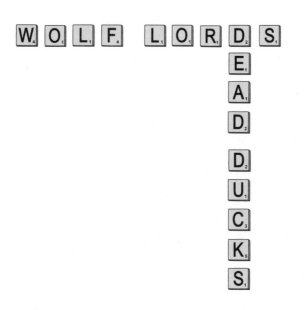

Messages   **Jason**

Today 6:56 PM

How's it going?

Not good. I'm gonna lose.

No you won't. You are
2 smart. 2 cute too 😄

Stop u r embarrassing
me. Won't be able to
concentrate. 😠

Messages **Jason**

Today 7:58 PM

I lost. 😭

No! 🙁

Yes. She killed me. I've been brutally slayed by a pigtailed freak named Harriet M. Welsch.

I will find her for you and destroy her. 😎 😇

I am so humiliated. I'm gonna hang up my Scrabble tile bag forever.

Nah. It's just a minor setback.

I'm serious. I hate Scrabble. 😠

LOL You do not. Just Harriet Welsch.

:D

Sleep on it. You'll change your mind in the M-O-R-N-I-N-G. 11. 🖼️

10. But who's counting. :D:D 💜

Tick. Tick. Tick.

We were in Travis's bedroom. Waiting.

Somewhere, deep in the bowels of the Sendak house, Conner was about to get some mind-blowing news.

Tick. Tick. Tick.

Bang! The door to Travis's bedroom burst open.

"You freaking won't believe this!" Conner shouted at us. "The Wolf Lords? They're done! Gone! They dropped out of school and left town!!!"

Travis leaned back against the wall. "Oh? Really?"

"Yeah, really! I just got a message from Z-Bar! He says some big heavy from down in the city showed up.

Covered with tats and pierced up the wazoo. Walked into Nino's like he owned the place.

"He goes, *So who's the man, here,* and Panzo goes, *You must mean me,* and the dude grabs Panzo by the collar and says, *Not no more.* 'Cause some big-time gang from the city has decided to set up shop and that man is their advance man, making sure the local talent won't be giving 'em any problems."

"No kidding," Travis said, in a voice like, *Pass the mustard.* He twiddled his ballpoint nonchalantly between his fingers like a mini baton.

Conner grabbed the pen from Travis's hand. "Are you not getting me, bro? The Wolf Lords are finished. Finished!"

Travis held up his fist to me. I bumped it.

"Good job," he said.

"Back atcha," I said.

Conner looked at Travis. At me. At Travis. At me.

"What the—"

"We've got some news for you too, Conner. Something even more interesting." Travis pointed to his desk chair. "Have a seat."

Conner gave him a blank look.

I scooted over and held the chair for him. "Conner? Please. Sit."

He sat. I turned the chair so Conner was facing the computer.

Travis, meanwhile, was tappity-tapping on the keys, rapid-fire.

A video frame came up on the monitor.

"Ready?" I asked him.

Travis nodded.

"Hold on to your hat, Conner," I said. "Prepare to be shocked. And awed."

Travis pressed *Play.*

SCENE: HOUSE INTERIOR. Shabby, sagging sofas. Pizza box on coffee table. Some red plastic cups scattered messily. Against one wall are some plant stands with UV lights over them.

SFX: POUNDING ON DOOR.

MR. BIG enters the room from another part of the house—the kitchen? Shaved head. Bushy straw-colored square beard. Leather vest. Black jeans. Death Metal T-shirt. He is heavily pierced and tattooed.

He opens the door. Two younger men enter. They are
Z-BAR and DRE DOG, heads of the Wolf Lords.

MR. BIG
Thanks for coming, boys.

Z-BAR
Er, our pleasure.

DRE DOG
Yeah.

MR. BIG
Sit. Sit.

He clears some biker magazines off the sofa. Z-BAR
and DRE DOG sit gingerly on the edge of
the seat.

MR. BIG
So you know why I invited you here, don't you?

Z-BAR
Not exactly.

MR. BIG
Wrong answer.

DRE DOG
Well...when your, er, friend? Came to the pizza place?

He told our boys something about new arrangements.
Made by, er, his associates? In the city?

Z-BAR
He meant you, right?

MR. BIG
(laughing)
You could say that. But not just me. I belong to an
organization. I'm sure you have heard of us.

Mr. Big cracks his knuckles. Makes a vroom vroom noise
with his mouth. And a revving gesture with his fists.

Z-BAR
Yes. We have. Sir.

MR. BIG
Then you know that we are a bunch of friendly fellers
who like to take our choppers for rides in the country,
and when we find a new place we like, well, we move
in. Make ourselves at home.

Z-BAR
Oh...

MR. BIG
And set up shop. 'Course, we don't like to have any
trouble. With, say, punk kids who think they own
the place.

DRE DOG
We're cool with working with you. Sir.

MR. BIG
Kind of you to say so, heh-heh. But we don't play
with amateurs, son.
(cracks his knuckles again)
Amateurs have a way of getting hurt. Badly.
(chuckles)
In fact, we'd prefer it if you boys got yourselves
out of the picture all together. I hear Florida is
very nice this time of year. All year.
Every year.

Mr. Big reaches under the couch. Brings up a
baseball bat. Dangles it from a meaty fist, letting it
swing back and forth, back and forth.

MR. BIG
Do we understand each other?

DRE DOG
(gulping)
Yeah. We cool with Florida. Very cool.

Z-BAR
Very cool.

END SCENE

When the video ended, Conner just kept staring at the screen.

"Holy crap," he breathed. "Can I watch that again?"

Travis hit *Play* again. Conner watched again, rapt. Dumbfounded.

"I can't believe this! Dre Dog and Z-Bar, man, they just caved. Like little girls."

Travis and I exchanged a look. Good thing Opal or Lu weren't here. They would have served him his head for supper.

Conner was still gawping, exclaiming, trying to make sense of what he'd just seen. "This is freaking something else...unbefreakingamazing."

Then he froze. Like a bunny in the lettuce, suddenly aware that the farmer is standing over him. With a rake.

He spun around and stared at us.

"How did you two get this vid?"

"Magic," Travis said with an ominous chuckle. A Beast-style chuckle.

Oh yeah—Travis was enjoying this. I was too. Turning the tables on Conner certainly had its charm. It was worth savoring the moment.

Conner's arm shot out. His fingers wrapped around Travis's throat.

"How did you get this vid?" he repeated, this time in a low, dangerous growl that made my hair stand on end.

I quit gloating. *Psycho* was the operative word when dealing with Conner, and we'd best not forget it.

"Let go of him, and we'll tell you," I said.

Conner let go.

I said, "We've upped our game, Conner. Now it's time to up yours. You have your phone on you?"

Conner looked at me like I was the crazy one.

"Call this number, then." I recited a number.

He dialed.

While he waited for the connection to click in, I said, "Do what the person on the other end tells you to do. Exactly. No deviations. If you do, all will be revealed. If you don't? Well"—I held up my own phone—"I've got Mr. Big on speed dial."

Conner listened as Jason gave him instructions over the phone.

"Got it…got it…"

Then he turned to us. "Seems I have to go collect your pal-sy Jason. And bring you fools along."

"Better hop to, then," Travis said.

We waited while Conner grabbed his keys and wallet. Then we followed him out to the used Neon he'd bought in December. With his ill-gotten gains.

Travis jumped into the front seat; I slid into the back. Right behind Conner, so I could lean my elbows on his seat top and bump him "inadvertently" (heh-heh) as I directed him to my house.

Jason was waiting for us on the front porch, a cheese-eating grin slapped across his face. He slid into the seat beside me and told Conner where to go.

Left at this street.

Right at that street.

After about the 45th turn, Conner said, "You're not taking me on some stupid kiddie wild goose chase are you?"

"You can let us out here, if you like," Jason said. "But then you'll never know the truth about that video. How we got it. And how we know what we know. And what it all means. To you."

Conner drummed his fingers on the steering wheel. Clearly considering his options. I knew he wanted to dump us out right there, on the doorstep of Kwikki-Lube Tire Center. To go back to the way things used to be, when he was our Master and had the control…

But those days were over, and Conner knew it.

We held the leash now.

"Make a left at the next stop sign," Jason said.

Conner turned left.

We drove for another ten minutes, heading first toward the north side of town, then into the industrial park, then back around again. Finally, we pulled up in front of a ramshackle house in the not-so-good part of town.

"Stop here," Jason said. "Turn off the engine."

Conner eyed the sagging front porch uncertainly. He ran his gaze over the broken lawn furniture, arranged like front-row seating for a zombie resurrection. The whole place oozed creepy.

"This looks like some kind of meth house, dude."

"And your point is?" Travis said.

"Trust me, kid, we don't want to go in there."

"Maybe not. But we are anyway. We have an invitation," Travis said. "You in particular."

Conner couldn't help himself. He gulped.

The look on his face was what you might call "supreme terror."

Heh-heh.

Jason led us up the crumbling concrete stairs, whistling the whole way like some kind of demonic pied piper. He rapped on the flimsy screen door, *knockety knock knock.*

Conner shifted his weight, one foot to the other, as we waited.

A lone squirrel *ch-chucked* pathetically in the trees. A car engine backfired in the distance.

Thick, heavy footsteps reverberated through the thick, heavy door. Someone very thick and very heavy was approaching it. Approaching us.

Mr. Big.

Conner gulped again. "Maybe we should reconsi—"

The door opened.

It was him—the Mr. Big from the video.

"Jason," he said.

"Eric," Jason said back.

Mr. Big pushed open the screen door and invited us in. He shook Jason's hand as we entered.

A square-jawed woman with purple-streaked hair emerged from the kitchen. She was wearing purple sweatpants and a purple T-shirt. The T had a picture of a grizzly with open, dripping jaws on it, and the slogan "Watch out, boys, Mama's comin'!"

"Hey, hon," she said to Jason. She kissed him on the cheek, then wrapped him in a—yes—bear hug.

She jerked her head toward Conner. "This the guy you told us about?"

Jason nodded.

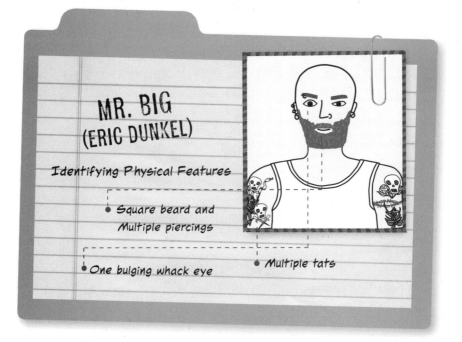

MR. BIG
(ERIC DUNKEL)

Identifying Physical Features

- Square beard and Multiple piercings
- One bulging whack eye
- Multiple tats

Assets: Scary demeanor. Top-level information access. 2-bedroom bungalow. Secret good nature, sense of humor. Superior acting experience, ability

Liabilities: Actual adult, sort of. Sense of responsibility, maturity.

Previous Missions:

☆ None

Status: Special Agent

She made a dismissive *humph*, then swept her hand toward the living room.

"So let's get this party started, then. Come on in!"

Conner gaped at Jason. He gaped at Eric. He gaped at everything.

"Close your mouth, Conner. You look like a tool when you let it hang open like that," Travis said.

Conner closed his mouth.

"Lemonade, anyone?" Eric asked. "I just mixed up a fresh batch. And I brought home some cookies from The Rolling Pin on my way home from work. Organic oatmeal-raisin—the best."

"Thanks, but no thanks," Travis said.

"I'm good," Jason said.

"Me too," I said.

Conner just sat and stared, guppy-like.

We shuffled over to the sofa and sank down into the squashy pleather. Conner, Jason, Travis and me, in a row.

Eric lowered his massiveness into the recliner across from us. Miss Purple, meanwhile, stood beside a sturdy plant rack. Arms crossed, hip cocked.

CHANDRA
AKA MISS PURPLE
(KAREN ARSENICO)

Identifying Physical Features

- Very dark purple lipstick and purple hair

Questionable fashion sense...purple fetish

Assets: Inexplicable loyalty to Jason Arsenico. 2-bedroom bungalow. Superior acting experience, ability

Liabilities: Actual adult, sort of. Sense of responsibility, maturity. Kinda weird.

Previous Missions: **Status:** Special Agent
✿ None

Eric cracked his knuckles. One. By. One. He had a seriously sick look in his eye. "So. Who wants to start this little reveal-all tale?"

Jason looked at me. I looked at Travis. Travis looked back at me. I looked back at Jason.

"I guess that's me, then," Jason said. "Conner, this man in front of you is Eric Dunkel. He is not a member of a biker gang. He is a research librarian at the community college over in Dryden. He also happens to be the boyfriend of my half sister, Karen." He waved his hand toward Miss Purple.

"Pleased to meet you, I'm sure," Karen said dryly.

"You took that video…" Conner said to her.

"Please don't interrupt," Jason said.

I stifled a laugh.

Jason continued, "You'd put us in a pretty pickle, Conner, with your extortion scheme. And none of us were amused. Not one bit.

"We figured out pretty early on that the only way we could get out of the clutches of the Wolf Lords was to convince them they had bigger problems than us. To do that, we'd have to be very smart, and very clever, and very sneaky. That's where these two guys came in. They happen to be all of those things. In spades."

Travis and I dipped our heads in acknowledgment.

"When those two put their heads together, you better watch out. They did, and what they came up with was incred.

"They proposed we run a 'sting.' An A1 scam, a hustle, a good old-fashioned con game of the first order. We would fool the Wolf Lords into thinking a biker gang was coming to town, and force them to think they had to get out of the extortion business ASAP unless they wanted to find themselves at the bottom of the Tuskageela River.

"Naturally, running a con game on this scale needed serious preparation. We'd need set, cast, script—the works."

"We turned to Jason's sister for help," I said. "She was great."

"Aw, thanks, Darren!" Karen leaned across and ruffled my hair. *Ick.*

"It turns out Karen and Eric are both really into cosplay. You know, dressing up, acting out roles and stuff? They go to these regular games sessions where

Eric is, like, a dragon slayer and Karen is a sorcerer-blacksmith-sword wielder."

"She's awesome," Eric said. "You should see what that girl can do with a 12th-century broadsword."

"Anyway," Jason said, "we described what we were thinking about to Karen, and she said that sure, they could help."

"Anything for my little bro," Karen said. This time she ruffled Jason's hair. His cheeks went red. "Besides, it sounded like some major fun. Putting the fear of God into some wannabe thuglets. And I loved the idea of acting the role of a biker chick. Because it's so me." She laughed.

"So together, we dreamed up this wackadoo plan to scare the living bejeebus out of the Wolf Lords," Jason said.

"And let's face it—you're one scary-looking dude, so it wasn't hard," Karen said, knuckling Eric's bald head. He didn't seem to mind.

Conner's eyes darted around the room. "So you set this whole thing up…making the house look like some biker pad…"

"It didn't take much, really," Eric said. "Neither Karen nor I are big on housekeeping."

"And those plants? Under the UV lights? They're not—"

Karen said, "No! 'Course not! What do you take us for? They're African violets! For the video, we stuffed some fake leaves in there with them. To make the place look more authentic. But come on, I'm no criminal. I'm a legal beagle by day, and a flower fanatic by night." She retrieved a plant from the stand and held it under our noses. "You see that there? That flower? It's totally unique. If I can get it to breed true, I'm going to name it after Eric. 'The Dragonslayer,' I'm gonna call it."

Conner clucked his tongue. Some color had come back to his cheeks, and with it, an air of insolence I found utterly unattractive.

He said, "Well, I must say. I am impressed. And not only with your lovely violets, Karen. Turns out my brother and his wee pals are more talented than I ever imagined.

"Now that I know you're so capable, I'm sure I can put your skills to use in the new Wolf-Lord organization, of which I am now, apparently, boss. Which I sincerely thank you for arranging. You've conveniently shaved about six months off my takeover schedule."

Conner got to his feet. "This has been most edifying and entertaining, but I really do have to go."

Eric grabbed Conner by his stringy hair. "Not so fast, basement boy." He shoved him back down into the pleather. It made a gassy *woomph* as Conner's butt sank into it.

"You haven't heard it all, Conner," Travis said. "Not yet."

"Nor seen all," I said.

Eric pulled his cell phone from the pocket of his jeans. "I've got the second video ready to play. Right here."

"Oh goodie," Karen said. She perched on the arm of the sofa, cradling the African violet like a baby. "This is the part I've been waiting for. The part where I'm the star."

Eric tapped his touch screen twice. He turned the phone's face toward us as our second video creation rolled.

SCENE: SAME HOUSE INTERIOR.
MR. BIG is talking to CHANDRA, who is watering the plants.

MR. BIG
I don't think we'll be hearing much from those punks.

CHANDRA
Nope. They practically wet their pants.

She laughs an evil laugh. She turns to face Mr. Big, holding the watering can in front of her in a curiously threatening way.

CHANDRA
How'd you know who to bring in, dude? We've only been here in Preston, like, two days. It usually takes you at least a week to figure out who the small-timers are.

MR. BIG
True. But this time I had some help.

CHANDRA
Oh?

MR. BIG
Yeah. Seems this kid spotted me. Out scouting or whatever. Imagines himself some kind of nefarious Snowden hacker spy, string-pulling, computer-geek god. Not sure how he found me but he did.

CHANDRA
Doesn't take a genius to figure out you're connected.

She points to his tats. Tugs on his square beard. He swats her away. She scowls, threatens him again with the watering can.

MR. BIG
Suppose not. Anyhows, he comes up to me at that dump diner and asks me straight out, like, if I need any info on the town. 'Cause, like, he's got it.

CHANDRA
Guy's got nerve.

MR. BIG
Guy's got stupid is what he's got. Anyhows, I say sure, I'll listen. And he spills that for a small fee he'll give up the names of all the players.

CHANDRA
What???

MR. BIG
So I says sure, and he give 'em up and I give him a C-note and he says he's at my service any time. And he freaking gives me his card. Can you dig that? His business card!

CHANDRA
What'd it say? Mr. Death Wish? Mr. No Hoper? Mr. Whack?

MR. BIG
Nope.
(He looks straight at the camera)

It just says, Conner Sendak. IT Professional.

END SCENE

Notes from Meeting with Travis, Jason, Conner, Eric and Karen (cont'd).

THHGFGH5458762-9 (cont'd). De-encrypted. 2/25.

"That's such b.s.! You know that!" Conner yelled. He tried to jump to his feet but was held fast by the squooshy[3] pleather.

"'Course it is," Eric said. "It's part of a scam, remember?"

"So that's just stupid, man! No need to be making stuff up and dragging my name into it."

"We disagree with that," I said. "Most heartily. We knew getting rid of the Wolf Lords was only our first step toward freedom from oppression. The second step was putting a stop to you."

---

3   TM* Word coined by Dirk Daring. Its use is legally protected by trademark. Squooshy.

"Think of this video as our insurance policy. Protecting us from you, Mr. Twenty-Five Bills a Week," Jason said.

Travis got to his feet and faced Conner. "Your little reign of terror is over, bro. If you make so much as a peep in our general direction about any of this, or try to lord it over me or anyone else ever again, we will send the video to Carson Thuen. Remember him? Z-Bar's little brother?"

Conner gaped at Travis.

"Z-Bar may have quit school, but Carson is currently a grade 8 student over at Northern. We're pretty sure that Carson will deliver this story of betrayal quick-quick to Z-Bar. Who we're also pretty sure will wanna come back—he's not in Florida, by the way; he just moved in with his dad over in Utica—and have a 'talk' with you once he hears it. Not to mention, I will personally deliver this piece of evidence to Mom and Dad, who will unplug your little electronics nest and slap you into military school so fast your head will spin."

"But wait—there's more, just like in infomercial land," Jason said. "Karen here has taken extremely detailed notes of all your shady activities. Like how you've been selling hot electronics? Online through Craigslist?

All the stuff the Wolf Lords stole in B and E's all over town?"

"I know quite a few cops who'd be very interested in that information," Karen said. "Very."

Conner's face went the color of wet ash.

"I think he's getting the picture now," Eric said pleasantly. "Not as dumb as he looks."

"Yeah. Close your mouth, Con," Travis said.

We still weren't finished though.

I reached into my jacket and pulled out a bulging black wallet.

A silver lightning bolt on the front. A huge wad of bills inside.

I threw it down on the coffee table. "I bet you'd like to know where this came from," I said.

Conner eyed it nervously, like it might jump up and bite him any second.

"That's Dre Dog's wallet," he said.

"Uh-huh," Karen said. "Eric here convinced him it was in his best interest to give us a 'finder's fee'—for finding Preston, ha-ha. That's the money the Wolf Lords extorted from Preston kids, and Northern kids too, since the beginning of the term."

Conner swallowed. "That's a lot of money…"

"It sure is. But that's just a portion of what they—and you—stole. Since September, we calculate they extorted three times that amount."

I plugged the numbers into my phone's calculator. Came up with a sum so large it made your heart drop a stitch.

I showed it to Conner. Heard, with utter satisfaction, his gasp.

Travis said, "And you've caused a lot of pain, too, you and your friends. So don't think we're done here."

"What do you want? An apology?" Conner said, jaw thrust high in the air.

Travis laughed. "Fat chance we'd get one from you. But even if we did, it would mean nothing. So let me spell it out for you: I want you to pay in the only way you know how. Cash. You're going to pay back every penny of that stolen money, and then some. Starting right now."

"I don't have that money! You know that, bro! It's all gone into my college fund!"

"I'm sure we can work out a payment plan," I said, touching more numbers on my calculator. "A weekly sum, plus, say, a small service charge?"

"Starting right now," Travis said. He held out his hand. "Fifty dollars, please. And Conner? Don't forget to say thank you."

Conner spluttered. "I'm supposed to *thank* you???? What the frick for?"

"For letting you live."

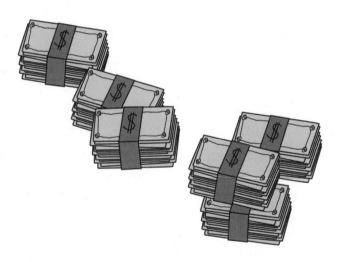

Spelling out the Truth.

Success was sweet. Yet I could not rest on my laurels. Not Dirk Daring, Secret Agent.

Having a team had made me stronger, more capable, than ever before.

But it had also made me more vulnerable. I risked betrayal at every turn. And never more than now, at the moment of my greatest triumph.

Two of our team had gone missing.

Where were they when we dragged the Beast from his lair and shone the light of our brilliance upon him?

M.I.A.

I would find them. And find them out.

Left, right, left, right, I scanned the scene. No one visible on the street. Just one light shining in the window of 12 South Park Drive.

Jewel's HQ.

Step by step, inch by inch, I made my way along the side of the house. There. A drainpipe. Ivy. Trellis.

A serious security lapse for an agent of Jewel's caliber.

A serious opportunity for Dirk Daring, Secret Agent.

Step by step, inch by inch, I hoisted myself up the drainpipe. As easy as climbing a ladder.

And there—my target. The lit window. Agent Jewel's bolt-hole.

I reached inside my flak jacket. I had stashed a specially constructed periscope in its secret pocket. With just one flick of my wrist, it would allow me to peep into the window from a safe distance.

Slowly, silently, I flicked my wrist and extended the periscope. The periscope's head nudged the window frame.

Once I put my eye to the other end, all would be revealed.

I peered.

There—inside the room.

One blond head—Agent Jewel.

One dark head—Agent Fury.

As suspected!

Together! Conspiring!

Their recent enmity a charade!

The unwelcome confirmation of my fears caused my hands to shake.

In an effort to keep the periscope still, I took a long, deep breath and held it.

Surprise, surprise: without my own sounds deafening me, I could now make out their voices. They were faint, yes. Very faint. But distinctly audible.

I took another breath and held it.

"Do you have the evidence?" I heard Agent Jewel say.

Exhaled.

Inhaled.

"…incriminating!" Agent Fury said.

Exhaled.

Inhaled.

"…got it. Right here. His fingerprints. I lifted 'em off a—"

Exhaled.

Inhaled.

"Waldo will put them in the cash folder. Dirk will be done," Agent Jewel said. "Bwa ha ha!"

My whole body went ice-cold. *I WAS BETRAYED!!!!!*

I slipped the periscope back into my jacket. Heart thundering, mind racing, I began my panicked descent.

ZZZHRIP! The sound of a sash window opening.

I froze.

Opal grinned down at me. Lucinda's own pink-and-purple Cheshire-cat grin gleamed from above Opal's left shoulder.

"Hey. We were expecting you," Opal said.

She pointed to an ivy leaf. Behind it, a camera. "Smile."

Lucinda yelled down at me, "We watched you the whole way. There's another camera showing the driveway."

"You didn't think Allegra Montefiore would let another spy sneak up on her so easily, did you?" Opal said.

I, Dirk Daring, was speechless. Caught in their twin beams of revelation.

"Don't just hang there, Darren," Opal said. "Come on inside. I made some cocoa. With marshmallows. There's a cup for you."

Sheepishly, I climbed back up the drainpipe. Grabbed onto the windowsill. Swung myself across the gap and clambered inside.

"How did you know—I mean, how did you know I'd be coming?" I said when I'd caught my breath.

"When we didn't show up for the big reveal, we *knew* you'd be suspicious," Opal said.

"It's kinda what you do, Darren. Suspect people," Lu said.

"It's not like I haven't had good reason," I said.

"True," Opal said. "But also not true. Don't you think part of the reason you can't trust people is because you don't trust them?"

"Huh?"

"I mean, if you always expect the worst of people, they'll live up to it."

I blew on the cocoa in the mug Opal handed to me. It didn't need me to—it had been sitting long enough that the marshmallows were nothing but a cool, waxy film on the surface.

"Yeah," Lu said. "That's it exactly. It's why I kept wanting to mess with your head. The way you looked at me all the time, like I was about to go gaga and do something stupid or crazy or mean made me want to do something stupid or crazy or mean. Sometimes I even did. Not proud about it." Lu looked away. "But there you go. Live and learn."

She brushed her hair out of her face. There was a ring on her right hand. One I recognized.

Jason's.

I never saw that one coming either.

"Last thing I remember, you and Lu weren't talking," I said to Opal.

Opal shrugged her shoulders. "I had it out with her. She said she made a mistake and was sorry. That was good enough for me. I can't manage having more than one giant problem in my life right now."

I knew she was thinking about Amber.

Lu said, "And you should say you're sorry too for not trusting us and creeping up here like some creepy stalker. And you think *I'm* weird. Seriously, Darren. Get a grip."

I bristled at Lu's words but then let my shoulders drop.

"I guess you're right. But why didn't you come? You both said you'd be there."

Opal gave me a long, hard, cool stare. "It just seemed like a boys'-club kind of thing. I mean, you and

Travis—you two really cooked this whole scheme up. It was your deal. And you and Jason—well, I just thought it was kinda cool to see you two acting like real brothers for a change. Doing something good together." Her eyes drifted away from me.

Amber again.

"So we decided to come here and wait for you. We figured you'd be here by 10 at the latest." Lucinda turned to the clock on the wall. It read *9:58.* "Right on schedule." She shook her head. "Too predictable for a good spy, Darren. You ought to shake things up a little. Anybody could scope you out."

I sighed. She was right again.

Lu said, "We were into a crazed game of Scrabble while we waited for you. Check it out."

There, on the floor, the Scrabble board was partly covered with words.

TURD

BOVINE

BLADDER

SNOTNOSE

NUT

"Lu's winning," Opal said. "Naturally."

"Yeah, well, I've had more practice. But all the really stupid words? They're hers. Come on, Darren. You can play too. Or keep score. Your choice."

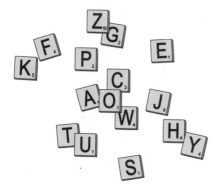

So there you have it. Mission accomplished.

And I don't mean putting an end to the Wolf Lords or kiboshing Conner's beastly business.

I mean the mission of surviving middle school.

For now, at least.

I confess that as I sipped my lukewarm cocoa, I struggled to make sense of everything that had happened since the start of the new year.

Travis and I were friends again.

Jason and I were acting like, well, real brothers. Whatever that means.

Strangest of all, there was the girl of my dreams. And me. Turns out we might have become a "thing."

How had it all happened?

Not a clue.

Watching Lu and Opal making words out of letter tiles, I thought about all the ways the words we used had messed us up.

It was careless words, cruel words, that had kicked off the fight between Opal and Amber back in the fall. Now that fight had developed a life of its own.

It was meddling words, talking-out-of-turn words— my own—that then made things even worse. Sure, my heart had been in the right place when I tried to talk some sense into Amber. But doing so wound up causing even more hurt between more people than I cared to think about. I should have just kept my nose clean and my lip zipped.

Then there was Lu. She had also talked out of turn. Her gossiping and tale-bearing had literally brought Opal and me to blows. She should have kept her lip zipped too.

And that was just the tip of the iceberg.

Every day, every one of us had engaged in an endless stream of sniping. Me, Travis, Opal, Jason, Lu. All of us, guilty.

We had used words like weapons—cross words, cross *swords*—to score points off each other.

We'd engaged in endless chirping. Jibing and counter-jibing. Snark and double snark.

In truth, we'd been so busy taking pokes at one another that we forgot to behave like *friends*.

Not exactly a recipe for happiness.

Sure, we all had history. We all had reasons to hold grudges, to look for ways to get even. But what was the point? Sometimes you just had to let stuff go. Endlessly rehashing old hurts just made things worse.

It was far better, I'd learned, to let sleeping dogs lie.

But when is the right time to speak? And when to stay quiet?

That's a good question, isn't it?

I'm afraid I haven't any answers. Not yet anyway. I'll still have to solve that puzzle somewhere down the line.

Luckily, I won't have to figure it out on my own.

Darren's Daily Journal.

At lunch today, I discovered a soggy square of paper between the mayo and the romaine on my turkey sub.

Rudolph rain dear stop hop dirk dark dork ok orc roc from firm farm jewel ring gem end [4]

I surreptitiously read the message it contained. Memorized it. Returned it to my sandwich. And continued eating.

It was the most delicious sub ever.

---

4   E3 code—read every third word only.

Ding dong. Door.

I peered through the sidelights. No one there.

Opened the door a crack.

There, stuck between the wooden door and the screen door, a package.

I retrieved it, checking left, right, left, right.

No one there. No one watching.

Or so it seemed.

I used a kitchen knife to carefully slit open the manila envelope.

Inside, a crudely laser-printed "newsletter." From the "Preston County Scrabble Society." It contained:

• A letter from the president of the society.

• A letter from the society secretary.

• A notice of the next meeting.

• An extensive report on the Scrabble Tournament held in the months of January and February.

The report included crude snapshots of the final boards of each championship game. With the order of words played. And the final scores.

There, in the middle.

Lucinda's matches.

Game 1:

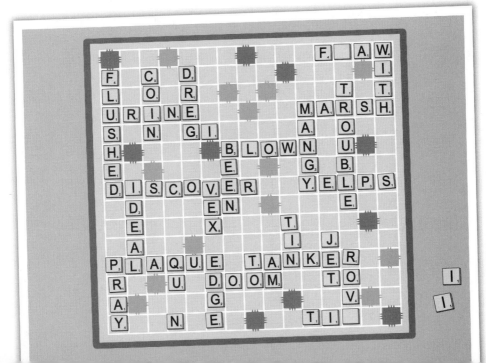

Game 2:

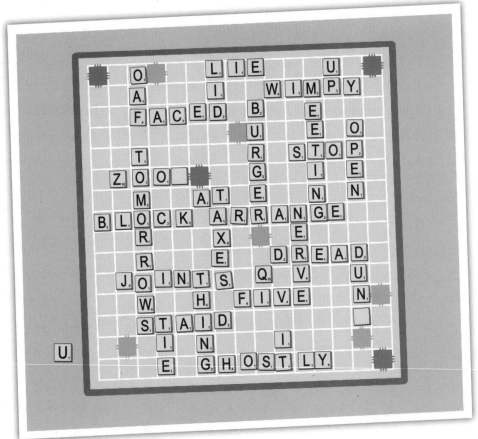

I left the open newsletter on the kitchen table and went to get my backpack. Retrieved my math text, *Patterns in Mathematics*, from it.

Between pages 32 and 33 lay a folded piece of newsprint. It had appeared there sometime between 800 hours and 1200 hours on January 25. I'd been holding on to it ever since.

I slid it from the book and laid it on the table beside the newsletter.

Game 1	Game 2
24	64
8	20
18	13
45	26
12	67
13	14

With utmost care, I matched the numbers on the newsprint to the words played by Lucinda's opponents that had the corresponding total points.

COVER (part of DIScover) 24
BEEN 8
BLOWN 18
FLUSHED 45
URINE 12
TROUBLE 13

My stomach clenched as the message became clear: *Your cover has been blown. You've been flushed out! And urine (you're in) trouble.*

Hurriedly, I matched the numbers to the words played in the second game—again, by Lu's opponent. The opponents, I now knew, were my colleagues in conspiracy.

ARRANGE 64
MEETING 20
BURGER 13
JOINT 26
TOMORROW 67
FIVE 14

A meeting's been arranged at your burger joint. Tomorrow at five.

I took the newsletter and the paper scrap over to the fireplace. Drew a long match from the box beside it. Moved the fire screen aside and placed the papers inside the grate.

Then I set them on fire. I watched the flames burn away every scrap of evidence while I contemplated the outcome of tomorrow's 5:00 PM rendezvous.

Somehow, I didn't think it would be pretty.

Messages	**Jason**

Today 7:28 PM

It's done. I sent the $.

The $ from YKW?

👍 Kids Help Phone will do good things with it. 📱

😊

PRESTON PRESTIGE

WINNER OF C.S. LEWISH PRIZE ANNOUNCED!

$5,000 Grant and a Trip to Oxford, England, for a Stellar Preston Student!

BY LUCINDA LEE, STAFF REPORTER

At a board meeting last night, Principal Nathaniel Lipschitz announced that the winner of the Doctor C.S. Lewish Prize for an Outstanding Student in a Tecumseh Head school was a Preston student! The prize comes with a $5,000 grant and a trip to attend summer courses for youth at Oxford University.

Of course, you must be dying to know who the winner of the award is. The recipient is Jason Arsenico, our very own Student Council president!!!!

Principal Lipschitz said, "Jason was selected for this award not only for his excellent academic record, but for his service to this school prin— er, school community this past term. His good work is much appreciated."

Jason declined to be interviewed for this article, saying he had studying to do, but this reporter knows it was really just because he was embarrassed by all the attention. Because no matter what people think, he's actually a very sensitive guy.

His stepbrother, Darren Dirkowitz, however, was delighted to speak on Jason's behalf.

"Jason is a very hard worker. He is very serious about his studies, and the Dirkowitz-Arsenico family is all really, really proud of him. We know he will make the most of this fabulous opportunity Principal Lipschitz has given him, and we are all looking forward to accompanying him to England this summer."

Helaine Becker is the bestselling author of more than sixty books for children and young adults, including the "enduring Canadian Christmas classic" *A Porcupine in a Pine Tree* and the giggle-inducing *Ode to Underwear*. She's also a three-time winner of the Silver Birch Award and a two-time winner of the Lane Anderson Award for Science Writing for Children. Helaine lives in Toronto with her husband and her dog, Ella. For more information, visit www.helainebecker.com.

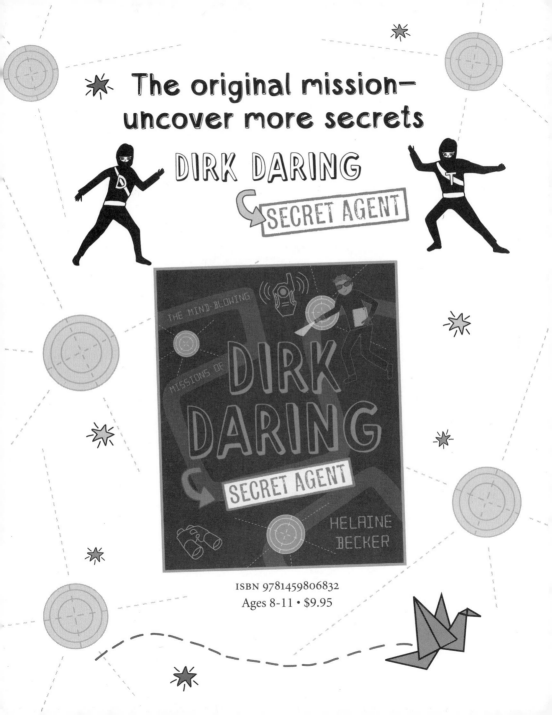

The original mission—
uncover more secrets

DIRK DARING
SECRET AGENT

ISBN 9781459806832
Ages 8-11 • $9.95